Death out of Season

Also by Meg Elizabeth Atkins

DEATH OUT OF SEASON

Meg Elizabeth Atkins

Constable • London

First published in Great Britain 2001
by Constable, an imprint of Constable & Robinson Ltd
3 The Lanchesters, 162 Fulham Palace Road,
London, W6 9ER
www.constablerobinson.com

Copyright © 2001 Meg Elizabeth Atkins

The right of Meg Elizabeth Atkins to be identified as the author
of this work has been asserted by her in accordance with the
Copyright, Designs and Patent Act 1988

ISBN 1–84119–433–6

Printed and bound in Great Britain

A CIP catalogue record for this book is available from the
British Library

To my friends
Margaret and Peter Lewis
with love

Prologue

The house was called Ferns. People who had known it in the past recognised the change. There were immovable features: wood panelling, moulded ceilings, wide, galleried staircase; and of the original furnishings a great deal remained: curtains, carpets – these of muted, restful shades. No, the transformation was not material – like double glazing or a refitted kitchen . . .

It was an insensible lightening. A buoyancy, as if a current of air had dislodged all the old presences – harsh, furtive, desperate – that for so long shaped the life in the house.

And it had not taken long. A few years. Not a lifetime.

A deathtime.

Outwardly, the house was unaltered. Stonework, gables, weatherboarding, Gothic windows – the madness of English architecture at its most interesting.

But then, the entire town of Clerehaven could be mad – at least, that was what DCI Sheldon Hunter came to think.

Chapter One

It came in like a sea-fret – a recurring local condition – except the sea was over twenty miles away. Mist rising from the deep gorge of the river, threading through the massive pillars of the viaduct, whispering about the steep streets of the winter town, revealing fragments: shifting, surrealistic . . .

Deserted boathouses at the water's margin, closed cafés, empty tennis courts, benches un-sat-upon affording scenic views.

This was the real magic of Clerehaven – out of season. Its fame and notoriety (deplored by entrenched residents) were lately earned. There had been, for so long, just the gentle rhythm of its days, composed, visibly, of leftovers: the shell of a castle, the remains of an abbey, the ruins of a manor house . . . All the decrepitude that should have allowed it to sink into the slumber of a forgotten English town. Had it not been for Alfred Lynchet. And the Toddies.

Early Saturday morning, the streets deserted, the shops unopened, Inez Bryant set out on her walk. A brisk ten minutes brought her to the door of old Mrs Hanks', which stood straight up from the pavement on high, narrow steps. The door opened, minimally, to a glimpse of a dressing-gowned figure, a smile too early in the morning to contain teeth, 'Hallo, Inez, dear.' And a small dog shot out, trailing its lead.

Compact body, short busy leg at each corner, dense, dun-coloured coat, long-snouted face. Mysterious components went into its breeding – something of a Jack Russell; a great deal of armadillo, Inez suspected.

'Well, where to this morning?' she would ask softly. It lifted its sweet, intelligent face. It knew they would walk three to four miles. It knew she had biscuits in her pocket.

Set into a scoop of cliff, looking down upon the broad, slow-moving River Clere, across to the viaduct, Clerehaven had nowhere to expand, except at its highest level, the Stray – the precipitous open ground to the west of the town. Some enterprising developer would have seized on this but for the Moreland family, who intended to keep Clerehaven firmly in its grip and were too rich to be coerced, bullied or bought off. Charles I had made the original gift of land to Lord Moreland (in appreciation of Lady Moreland's favours) under the impression he had given away a bit of Wales, his gonads functioning more efficiently than his geography.

Inez made her way up to the Stray so that she could have a view of the town descending on its many levels as the fret, shifting and moving, took away vistas, yielded glimpses here and there – as if the bones of the town were showing through. Then came the alchemical moment when the mist dissolved and it was all revealed: worn stone, painted stucco, old brickwork; trees and gardens, bowling greens, a corner shop, a grandiose gateway, a labourer's sturdy cottage; roads twisting, pathways appearing, turning back on themselves.

Afterwards, on the way back, they took a tour through High Town, appropriately named for its location, the loftiness of its old houses, its soaring trees. In deep gardens, behind high hedges and ranges of shrubs, summerhouses awaited their season. Tennis courts –

yes, even in 1990 – with their far-away echoes of Eton-cropped girls, epicene young men, tea on the lawn, curtseying servants . . . all the ghosts of High Town.

And then, Ferns. No house pre-dated the middle 1800s; Ferns had its own, undiscoverable timescale: architecturally both superb and potty, it was visible evidence of lives lived in it by secretive, arrogant people.

It had possibly, now, to Inez's eyes, reached its peace, with only Nella Lynchet left of the family – she might have odd bedfellows in the Toddies but they were providing her with a lifestyle she could never have looked for as an ugly child, a plain girl, a fat spinster.

Nella, with no resource but loyalty, had never been heard to breathe a word of criticism of her selfish, pompous brother, Alfred; her terrifyingly autocratic grandmother, Georgina Lynchet. But Inez, who found her difficult to like, felt the random heart-tug of fellow feeling that would have astonished Nella, had she known of it. Inez could read the muffled anguish in Nella's subservience, her need to placate, apologise, recompense. Continually, publicly, put down – *Nella, you were born a fool, like your mother* – Nella's good manners, ironically drilled into her by Grandmother Georgina, ensured she would never speak out in her own defence against the appalling old woman.

As for Inez, somewhere in her growing up she had found the strength to take a stand against her bullying mother. Her parents' marriage had been catastrophic, ensuring a wretched (unnoticed by them) childhood for her. Her mother fed upon aggression, dominance and paranoia. Jettisoning Inez's father, she married a second time and, when Inez was sixteen, accused her of carrying on with her stepfather and threw her out. The accusation was completely unjustified. Inez's stepfather, a sweet, ineffectual man, secretly pushed money into Inez's pockets when she left with her suitcase and rucksack. She never saw him, or her mother, again. She managed with help from friends and temporary shelter from her cousin and best friend, Mary Weller, who lived in Clerehaven. Coping with uncomplained hard times, Inez got through art college and, determinedly single, endured, succeeded. She had her career teaching and practising interior design. To her astonishment, when she was in her forties, she married.

She was wife number two; for Joe she was the gold at the end of the rainbow . . . Too short. Too late. The rainbow faded. Disappeared. Joe died of cancer, rapidly, painfully. But why in the name of God should he leave her with a freight of relatives: in-laws, stepchildren, aunts, uncles, nieces? She had never wanted any of them; after her destroyed and isolated childhood she could never grasp what families were about, why her late husband's should need to congregate, reminisce, gossip – a non-stop, nerve-racking cacophony of cheerful exchanges, all as beloved Joe was being lowered into the grave. Why should they not? Perhaps this was what was important – this *stuff*, this hugger-mugger of the commonplace. How could she, a loner, ever tell?

After Joe's death it became impossible for her to remain in their home in Cornwall. There was too much shared, too briefly, now forlorn – this was when Clerehaven indeed became a haven. Her dear Mary, dying of a stroke a year before Joe, willed to Inez her Rumpelstiltskin house, hidden away in the heart of the steep town. All the contents went to various friends, relatives, charities; Mary, with loving prescience, knew that when Inez moved into the house she would require a shell, a hollowed-out life to fill.

This was where, widowed, Inez sought to escape all Joe's relatives. An absurd optimism . . . The younger ones, unstoppably breeding, were particularly persistent. They kept turning up with babies who had to be instantly pottied or breast-fed, whose necessities spread a trail through the house. Inez, literally tripping over bundles of nappies, blankets, woolly animal things,

9

packs of food, thought dazedly of Africa, of strapping black women, naked baby on thigh – innocent of the blandishments of Mothercare.

She really did not know what to do with Joe's family; she tried, but any meaningful communication was beyond her. In a way she could never define she knew she did not exist for them: they talked around her, above her, beyond her, never meeting her eyes, never addressing her directly. Nobody had ever said a word about her lack of relatives, any allegiance she might have when theirs was so labyrinthine. How could she explain herself? She settled for cunning, which happily coincided with truth. Her house was small – only two bedrooms. Parking was restricted. She was scarcely accessible in winter . . . Bugger them, they wanted to come in summer. She began to pretend she was going on an extended tour of somewhere; a cruise. Weeks. Months. If – with the tenacity of the unwanted – they did turn up, she simply hid. They had maddening persistence, going round the house looking through windows, rattling doors. Once, shell-suited parents and four rampaging children picnicked in her garden – *She'll be just out shopping, we'll wait* . . . They had a car loaded with luggage. Trapped upstairs, what could she do?

She telephoned her friend, Sam. Shortly afterwards, he appeared in her garden with a story about her being rushed to hospital with a dangerously infectious disease. They left, precipitately. Later, he asked, 'Didn't they send a get-well card?' She muttered, 'Oh bugger off.' She hadn't much idea who they were and, so far, they had not turned up again.

Chapter Two

Down in the town, after she had delivered the armadillo back to Mrs Hanks, Inez made her way through quiet streets towards the one shop that would be open at that hour. On the sudden, startling opening of vistas, the cramped road gave way to a small, elegant square where a Victorian shelter stood, sturdy and practical, built to last for ever, its seats facing the four points of the compass, its wrought ironwork a burst of frivolity.

It was there Sam came upon her, crouching down by the seat, making herself as small as possible.

'Inez, what are you doing?'

For reply she reached up, grabbed him, pulled him down beside her.

He said, 'Not Joe's marauding family?'

'No, Jaynie Turner. There, talking to Mrs Arbuthnot.'

'Ah . . .'

Jaynie Turner, following her divorce, had moved from Chatfield to Clerehaven two years before. To everyone it seemed much, much longer.

She was in her early fifties and the entire course of her life was written all over her radiant prettiness: winner of the Beautiful Baby competition, enchanting child, exquisite girl, glamorous woman. As her dazzling presence was her passport, she had never seen the point in paying regard to anyone's feelings. Nerve-racked people muttered, *Why doesn't the stupid woman call herself Jane?*

Somebody once asked her.

Because, she answered, wide-eyed, as if it were only too evident, she had always been Daddy's Little Princess, little Jaynie. And because, as it was also only too evident, she needed the dispensation of the diminutive to behave badly, be selfish and vain and hurt people with cruel comments. But then, there was always the smile behind the beautifully manicured hand, the luxuriantly lowered lashes, the girlish giggle; never having moved on from the pampered and adored province of childhood, she knew she would be forgiven.

From their hiding place, Inez and Sam watched her making gestures towards herself: flowing, curvaceous. 'Oh, God, another bloody new frock,' Inez breathed.

Sam said, 'Well, I don't think she's asking Mrs Arbuthnot about her sciatica.' He was irredeemably practical. 'Listen. Suppose she walks round here and finds us.'

'We'll pretend we've lost something.'

He had a precise turn of mind, entirely appropriate to his work poring over minute differentiations in grasses at the Plant Research Institute. It did occasionally make people short with him, which he good-naturedly overlooked. 'Um . . . What exactly . . .?'

'One of your contact lenses.'

He thought about this for a moment before pointing out, painstakingly polite, that he didn't wear them.

'Oh, *all right*. My ear-ring.' She took one off, stuffed it in her pocket.

'Now what?' he asked.

'Let's look . . .'

They peered over the dividing partition. Jaynie had disappeared.

'Where were you going?' Inez asked.

'To have a walk with you and the armadillo, but I was too late.'

'Oh, I'm sorry. That would have been lovely. Let's go and get our papers and then come and have breakfast.'

This called for caution. Alert for the least sign of a lingering Jaynie, they made their way – flattened against buildings, sprinting across openings, peering and dodging back from corners.

When they had filtered into the shop, the newsagent (an imperturbable man) exchanged pleasantries, served them, watched the manner of their leaving with resignation.

Poised in the doorway, Inez said, 'We'll just have to make a break for it . . .' So they raced: Inez, a tall, stately woman with tousled brown hair, a broad, serene face, eyes full of laughter. Sam, elegantly casual, streamlined as a whippet, following her pounding Doc Martens, allowing her – twenty years his senior – to win.

It was not long before they reached their destination. The seven-foot high, weathered, exquisitely carved oak gates, always standing open; the name plate: Cremorne. Private.

It was a secret place at the heart of the town, people walked, drove past without realising it was there. In the 1700s there had been a farm, outbuildings. Then, when through the slow evolution of social life the farm became redundant, a spacious house of great charm was built upon its shell. The outbuildings became assorted dwellings – somebody, in 1930, built a perfect Metroland bungalow. By the time gas and electricity arrived, there were five houses and gardens set amongst the foliage and gravel paths, privacy and community. No one knew who had given Cremorne its name, or why, or who was responsible for the glorious gates.

They fell into her house, breathless with laughter. Inez gasped, 'It's Nella I feel sorry for.'

'Is Jaynie still pursuing this idea of their being related?'

'Of course, what else has she got to do?'

'Is there anything in it, do you think?'

'It's very doubtful. Nella is resisting the idea to the

death, who can blame her? But *Jaynie* is amassing all this
evidence . . .'

'Is it evidence?'

'What? Well, it's um – things she's finding out, reading old letters, looking at old – Sam, that's an odd thing
to ask.' Realising as soon as she'd said it that it wasn't;
he had an analytical mind, devoted to detail; she was
slapdash, leaping from one assumption to the other.

He said, 'I've just never fathomed how a woman with
the IQ of a tea bag ever got started on such a project –
never mind shutting up and sitting down and diligently
researching –'

'Ah, yes, I see. Come on. Kitchen. And I'll tell you.'

Chapter Three

They made breakfast companionably and lavishly, a feast with all the mad pleasure of the forbidden: buttered eggs, sausages, fried potatoes, mushrooms, crusty bread, a jug of fragrant coffee.

Sam had known Inez since he was a child; her house, with its enfolding calm, always held a special welcome for him. Although he had been brought up in Chatfield, he remembered his mother bringing him to visit her friend, Mary Weller, and Inez, her cousin, had often been there.

Inez explained about Jaynie. 'It was after the divorce –'

'Yes, he went off with a teenager or something, didn't he?'

'No, dear heart. He went off with a woman at least eight years older than himself, plump and motherly and dowdy.'

Sam stopped setting out their places at the big kitchen table and stared at her. 'I never knew that. I thought – well, she's always so bitter about husbands who dump their wives for younger models.'

'Of course, bitter because it didn't happen to her. He's a really nice chap, Arthur. I think he just got cheesed off living up to her expectations. He wanted to put his slippers on, wear old cardies, potter in his greenhouse. She'd never stand for that.'

'God, no,' Sam said, awestruck at the thought.

'So, yes, he took his chance of happiness when it came

along . . .' And he had, during thirty years of married life, fulfilled his obligations: showy house, children's education, exotic foreign tours, smart holiday villa somewhere, social status. Who could blame him for settling into the arms of his undemanding, comfy mistress? His children didn't. They had their own lives, all they wanted was to be left alone to get on with them but Jaynie, enraged, set about making the divorce as ferocious as possible and life hell for everyone. Her husband was a beast, her children disloyal, her replacement an old tart. *Yes, yes,* said her friends, *you're so brave, dear.* She was concentrating so hard on being beautiful in distress it took quite a while for her to realise her friends were getting far too much enjoyment out of feeling sorry for her.

She stopped making scenes; became an unremitting nuisance. Her ex-husband and children had assured her they would do everything they could to help her through this difficult period; very well then, let them. In a very short time she had exhausted everyone with her demands for attention, threats of suicide, telephone calls, histrionic performances in Sainsbury's, frantic messages, midnight appearances.

'They had to find her something to *do*, you see,' Inez said to the fascinated Sam. 'She was in the process of buying a house here – making it as long-drawn-out and catastrophe-prone as she could, naturally. They had a house in south Chatfield –'

'*South* Chatfield. There's posh,' Sam murmured.

'Yes, very. She insisted on having it as part of the divorce settlement, then changed her mind. Said she didn't have to put up with the pity of her friends. Can't say I blame her, they're a pretty poisonous lot.' So, Inez went on, she decided to live in Clerehaven, where she had been born and spent her early years – 'close to my roots'. It was this, Jaynie's ex-husband told Inez, that gave the family the idea, more or less spontaneously. They enrolled her in a local history course. It was a

16

desperate measure, he admitted, and they hadn't much hope it would work, but it might give her something to think about for a while and stop her driving everyone insane.

It succeeded amazingly. Jaynie had always had a sense of herself as someone special, here was a chance to prove it. In no time at all she managed to convert the study of the doings and beings of Clerehaven's more recent past into the closest possible scrutiny of herself. It was, also, an opportunity to ferret and pry and, for a woman who hated to be alone, an excuse to foist herself on other people. The – often strained – goodwill of friends, neighbours, acquaintances, ensured it was some time before anyone realised how relentlessly Jaynie was using her researches to refurbish her ego.

She took the opportunity to refer, as frequently as possible, to the unsubstantiated claim that somewhere, on her mother's side, her family had a connection with the Lynchets. It was plain it gave her status. For one thing, the Lynchets claimed to be an old, if not *the* oldest established Clerehaven family – but no one had ever been quite sure what was meant by that and as it was Grandmother Georgina Lynchet who made the claim no one dared ask. It was true they had lived at Ferns in High Town for as long as anyone could remember. Also, it was understood that Grandmother Georgina had at one time been headmistress of some prestigious girls' school. There had long ago been a Grandfather Lynchet, whose passing Georgina had never found it necessary to regret, although she dragooned everyone into regarding him with great respect: a man of the highest probity and distinction. Government service was reverentially implied.

Grandfather Lynchet. That was the first punctured pretension – although no one then realised Jaynie was set on a wrecking course; and no one could imagine what the outcome would be.

*   *   *

An amiable social occasion: fund-raising for the Water-man Disability Centre. Just a few words from a beauti-fully caring and careworn woman. Sherry and delicious home-made savouries. General conversation, turning – how could anyone trace the source of the subject? – to the Lynchets.

'*Grandfather* Lynchet. *Heavens . . .*' Jaynie's voice, always unpleasantly off-pitch, became strident when she was excited. 'No, he worked for the Council. Sani-tary department. I mean, you could say he was a *local government inspector* because he inspected lavatories and things. I mean *lavatories . . .*' The giggle, the sweeping-eyelash glance, assessing reaction: *Didn't you know?*

Strangulated, disbelieving silence.

Lavatories.

Fortunately, Nella was not present. Many people there knew her lifetime's humiliation at the hands of Grand-mother Georgina; the consensus was: For God's sake let's all just shut up. But would Jaynie, self-absorbed, tactless and spiteful, shut up?

No . . .

She had discovered a source of power: the legitimacy of her 'research', which gave her ascendancy in a com-munity where she might otherwise have been treated just like anyone else. Tirelessly inquisitive, she bided her time until another occasion (by then everyone, recognis-ing the signs, had learnt to snap into a social reflex: gritting teeth, feigning deafness, loudly changing the subject).

This time Jaynie had Grandmother Georgina in her sights. She would never, in the lifetime of the old woman, have dared to undermine the pretensions of the Lynchets. No one would. Once again, Nella was not present.

'Headmistress? Headmistress? Heavens, no. She helped out in the kitchens – Lady Marchant's Orphans' School – yes, I have *documentary* evidence. I'm very thorough in my research. Yes, her name on the pay sheets . . . and the copy of a letter, here, saying how efficient she was organising – food – things – saving so much money . . .' The flourishing of her impressive research file, a gold-tasselled pen. And a silence, spreading around her, which even she was forced to apprehend, although not to grasp.

That dreadful old woman, in the history of the world, might be ridiculed – but not publicly, in the society where she had moved, by this relentlessly trivial woman. Jaynie would have professed to understand nothing of this, had anyone asked her. No one did. Inez said to her special friend Dora Hope, 'She can do her wide-eyed bit till she splits open – she knows she went too far.'

'Oh, yes, absolutely. It's Grandfather Lynchet and the lavatories all over again. She expects everyone to join in the laughter. And when no one does – well, her justification is that no one has a sense of humour.'

'*Sense of humour* . . . Door . . .' (At the beginning of their acquaintance, before it became a friendship, a misreading of signatures resulted in their afterwards calling each other Door and Index.) 'Look, the only things she bloody laughs at are whoopee cushions and joke turds.'

'I rest my case. How many people – tactfully – have tried to make her understand that being so brutally frank about the Lynchets won't do anything for her popularity?'

Inez gazed wordlessly at her.

Dora sighed. 'Exactly. Complete waste of breath. Jaynie's only form of self-defence is to turn on what she incessantly pursues. Ever since Nella saw her off she's become so spiteful, the other day she said the Lynchets were nothing special and whoever heard of anyone claiming superiority just because they were named after a ditch.'

'Hasn't anyone told her a lynchet's an ancient field system?'

'What would be the point?'

Silently, they brooded on the basic common sense of this before mentally shifting gear to consider the other reason why Jaynie had, so to speak, sunk her teeth into the underbelly of the Lynchets. The kudos of transferred fame, the casual claim to association with a household name.

The Toddies.

It could only be said they were an aberration. They did not belong to Clerehaven, they did not belong to the haughty and fastidious Lynchets; their element was the super-orbiting popularity of a television soap, with all the hype, artefacts, ancillary publications, souvenirs and locations that that meant. There were – sown from their dragon's teeth and sprung from the gentle earth of Clerehaven – Auntie Vi's Tearooms, river launch trips complete with 1930s knees-up, Uncle Ern's Local (sing-alongs every Saturday), a Toddies' Trek and, in prospect, according to rumour, a Toddies' Experience.

It had happened in a few years. And all because of Alfred Lynchet.

The late Alfred Lynchet.

At the time when the Toddies were beginning to bed themselves into the nation's viewing psyche, Inez said to a friend, a successful, hard-working novelist, 'Well, look. Alfred. He's always written, anything, poems, reminiscences, local history. I know because we both do the circuit of small societies. And he never misses an opportunity to bore us to bloody death with his readings –'

'From what?' Her friend interrupted bracingly. 'Inez, he writes crap and pays for it to be published in shitty little magazines.'

'Well, yes, I must say that sounds about –'

'And now he's hit a winning streak. He got a toe-hold with an agent, somehow – furthermore, one who just happened to know Dee TV were on the lookout for something to replace that thingy series – vet, or something. Independent Telly are contractually bound to produce a certain quota of locally based programmes, including drama. What he had to offer just caught someone's commercial instinct. It happens. We all think, Christ, let it happen to me. Only it sodding doesn't.'

But, Inez thought, what was astonishing about all the years she'd been forced to listen to Alfred's pontifications on moral values, local culture, literary insights, was that there had never been a mention of the Toddies until a year before his death when, amazingly, he produced a series of short stories that went straight into the conveyor belt of agent, TV production company, prime time viewing. The medium was voracious; the programmes were recently networked in the United States, distributed – incomprehensibly – in Finland and Greenland, and lately, Inez had heard, sold to Japan. She was left dazedly considering how 1930s characters of quintessentially English comic gentility would go down in any of those alien locations.

After Sam left to go about his own concerns, Inez settled before the fire with the newspaper and her feet up, but she was not inclined to concentrate. The early, bracing walk up on the Stray, the gossip with Sam, turned lazily in her mind, gently collided with a recollection. Two – three years ago? 1987 or thereabouts.

It was a day she had walked over to neighbouring Byehaven (four miles, via the Stray, footpaths and open land. Seven by road.) to lunch with a friend.

She returned just as dusk was stealing over the Stray, the town lying below in an elegiac light. Just as she was ready to turn from the track and begin her descent, she saw Nella's Citroën 2CV parked farther on, dangerously close to the toppling chasm overlooking the river.

She halted. She could make out the darkened silhouette of Nella at the driver's seat. She could not think why Nella should sit there alone, motionless. Instinct told her there was something catastrophic, hidden . . . She approached hesitantly. Nella, oblivious, stared straight ahead; the image of someone destroyed.

Inez tapped on the window. Slowly, the fat face turned towards her, the eyes unfocused.

'Are you all right?' Inez asked gently.

The window wound down. Partially, reluctantly. 'Leave me alone, Inez.'

'Yes, yes, do forgive me.' Drawing back a few paces. Pausing. 'But . . . is there anything I can . . . Look, what about coming home with me and we'll have a cup of tea –'

'Oh, for God's sake leave me alone.'

Wordlessly, Inez retreated.

She knew about despair, how it needed its aloneness from which, with fortune, came the strength to face the next day, and the next . . .

She knew Grandmother Georgina was ill and Nella was going through a hard time; and it had not really been all that long since her brother, her only sibling, had died – an unlooked-for, violent death.

All the same. Nella, permanently apologetic about her very existence, had the occasional high manner, stopping just short of arrogance, but she had been drilled in courtesy, it was out of character for her to be so rude.

There was nothing to do, so Inez made her way home, spent an uneasy hour, then walked up to High Town and casually approached Ferns. She lingered at the double gates. Everyone was tucked away at home, having sherry, supper. There was no one to see her lift the catch and slip into the drive.

Ranges of bushes. Trees, dense hedges on either side of the house . . . She stepped on to the grass to save crunching the gravel. Moments later she was saying to herself it was surprising how deep you could get into someone's garden in the dark.

A curve in the drive and the house came into view. Her attention was at once taken by a lighted, half-open window. It was the drawing-room, she knew it from uncomfortable social occasions: a cold, gloomy, people-hating place. There was a glimpse of Nella, approaching the window; behind her the seated monolith of Grand-mother Georgina. Then the window clamped firmly shut, the curtains were drawn.

Go home, Inez. Nella has not, you have the evidence of your own eyes, driven her little tin car over the cliff into the river. What in God's name made you think she would?

So there's nothing to do. Just go home, Inez.

Chapter Four

The Friends of Clerehaven met on Thursday evenings at the Memorial Hall. Nella Lynchet, who belonged to everything, was not punctual. For one thing, the meetings never started on time; for another, as Grandmother Georgina so frequently said, only common people were punctual.

Grandmother Georgina's opinions, strictures, precepts and prohibitions stuck to Nella like burrs. She could, from time to time, remove one – always with the slightly uncomfortable sense that she was removing, along with Grandmother's exacting rules, some particle of herself. That was the difficulty, because for all the wretchedness of being bullied and ridiculed she had at the same time been relentlessly drilled into a sense of impeccable social superiority. As her grandmother said to anyone within hearing: 'If Nella hasn't the wit to be grateful to me for anything else, she can at least appreciate I have taught her faultless conduct.'

All right. Only its applicability was not nearly so useful as Grandmother claimed (the correct way to address a bishop had little place in Nella's life), but argument was out of the question – she had never known any law but Grandmother Georgina's and that was absolute. (It was true that in the old woman's final illness Nella said most of the things she had always wanted to say, but Grandmother was by then beyond comprehension and there ceased to be any satisfaction in telling the truth to someone who was incapable of understanding it.)

Nella and her brother Alfred came to Clerehaven from Dorset as children, after a boating accident that took their parents' lives. Alfred, the elder by five years, could remember his mother and father, retrieve fragments of early childhood; Nella could not. She had never known what it was to live anywhere except Clerehaven, with Alfred and Grandmother Georgina. Growing up, she slipped into place as the humblest and least considered member of the household. Alfred, of course, was always the object of his womenfolk's unstinting admiration – a reward no more than his due.

At Grandmother's insistence, they went into local government – safe and respectable, besides, their characters were so conditioned to the anxiety of doing the right thing they scarcely noticed the transition from home to work. Nella's status was humble; she accepted Alfred's as prestigious, even though common sense indicated it was not, but Nella, a true Lynchet, had an amazing capacity for self-deception.

In her late thirties she had her only love affair, although she was so innocent her notion of love had nothing to do with the exploitation she endured. He was a small, dapper, fast-talking salesman, plundering her body in a way that bewildered and repelled her but, as she assumed she represented sexual desire, she bore the hasty fumblings and gruntings with resignation.

She was secretly amazed that neither Grandmother nor Alfred attempted to discourage her. It was true 'the boyfriend' was seldom allowed over the doorstep and never invited to family occasions. Grandmother managed, always, to call him by the wrong name and Alfred's loud remarks – *out again this evening . . . he must be keen . . . when do we expect an announcement?* – were made with a faintly detectable sarcasm. But she took as a sort of encouragement their smiles, whispers, knowing looks, which remained unchanged even though he was plainly humiliating her and continued – if anything, became more evident – after he dropped her. Their sympathy then was of the bracing it-was-obvious-he-was-up-to-no-good variety. In her desperate hurt she suggested timidly that they might have warned her, to be told by Grandmother that if she wasn't capable of looking after herself at least they thought she'd have the sense to look after her money. Her salary was adequate for her modest needs, she always saved from it, and she had a small inheritance from her parents; he had managed to con and bully her out of most of it. That was what had attracted him; and they always knew. Her pathetically failed love affair finished up as just another triumph for Grandmother.

Even after her death, so powerful was her personality, Grandmother Georgina continued to stride through the corridors of Nella's memory. Tall, gaunt as a hungry eagle, with fierce eyes that saw everything, clothes that never altered, long and dark and skinny, three generations out of date – although she was much too distinguished for anyone to point this out to her. After her death Nella found wardrobes and chests and cupboards full of them, musty with the smell of an old body, by their very volume claiming tenacious occupancy of Ferns.

Without hesitating, Nella made a bonfire in the garden and burnt them all. It was her first act of independence, justified by a wholly new sensation of bitter and vengeful satisfaction: what else could she do with them? A charity shop would scarcely be appropriate for a woman who had never had the least charity toward anyone.

With Grandmother's death she was alone, Alfred having met his end, with shocking violence, two years previously, killed by a hit and run driver who was never traced. With the sense of posterity instilled in him by Grandmother Georgina, he left his worldly goods to his sister Nella (they were, at the time he drew up his will, pretty trifling). More significantly, he made his grand-mother and Nella his joint literary executors.

Joint – it went without saying – was a courtesy desig-nation. Grandmother Georgina moved into the driving seat of Alfred's accelerating reputation – nagging his agent, terrorising the production team, grandly accord-ing interviews. Only her failing physical condition kept her from manhandling script conferences where, legally, owing to Alfred's forethought, she had a say. In all this, there was no question of the least whisper of Nella's voice being heard.

It did not last. Little more than a year after Alfred's death Grandmother Georgina recognised and con-fronted her own mental deterioration. Typically, she laid her plans; under no circumstances would she allow the name of Lynchet to sink into obscurity. There was only one thing to do: using what time she had left, she prepared Nella for the future. No, not Nella's future – who cared about that? *Alfred. His reputa-tion, his career . . .*

And so the Toddies passed into Nella's guardianship. Brought up in Grandmother Georgina's unforgiving exactitudes, she could not help feeling anything except a stunned distaste for these characters who called table napkins *serviettes* and to whom gracious living was embodied in a pink glass, musical cocktail cabinet. But . . . common as they were, they were also the source of Alfred's wealth and fame; and there was always Grand-mother Georgina's advice: 'Think of them as servants for whom you are responsible. It becomes quite easy in time.'

The Toddies, a rampantly sentimentalised 1930s fam-ily, were lovingly depicted down to the last detail. Mum, Marcel-waved, striving for gentility; pipe-smoking Dad in his Fair Isle pullovers, cherishing an image of himself as a bit of a rascal; assorted small Toddies, variously winsome or repellent. A large family of aunts, uncles, cousins, grandparents, in and out of scrapes. A fatherly policeman dealing clips on the ear to young scallywags. Recognisable Clerehaven locations for which most residents cursed Alfred. (Inez's friend Sam, a minutely informed reader of crime novels and watcher of hospital traumas, said, 'Honestly, I've never been able to understand their appeal. You can't say it's the stuff of human life. They've never *been* human.' 'I rather think that's the point,' Inez said.)

Nella's schooling in the management of these characters was unremitting; bludgeoned into her duty to Alfred – at first terrified – she found herself confronted by an amazing, undreamt-of circumstance. Power.

Power to carry out negotiations, conduct business with his agent, liaise with the television company, dictate terms to publishers and editors. Without knowing quite how it happened, she became an authority on every aspect of her brother's work: she judged competitions, appeared on radio phone-ins, gave talks on the social significance of what she insisted was a drama series but everyone else called soaps.

The old lady's baleful presence banished, Alfred's could be said to be enshrined. He had not been an academic, had no writing reputation; whatever had been on the horizon of his striving, no one ever knew. The reality was he had achieved a meretricious fame, with which his grandmother and his sister colluded, as something admirable. This hollow reputation had room for both of them: Grandmother Georgina fostered his memory and reputation – until it was Nella's turn. From the periphery of his life, excluded and ridiculed, she moved to the centre, came, by some process no one understood, to be acknowledged as his inspiration.

She gave up her modest job and with increasing confidence took to her new life, her evolving self – without managing ever to acknowledge any change had taken place. There was an existential aspect to this: what she came to understand of herself was that she had always been in control, interesting, positive. There was the trifling matter of her physical appearance, but she had forgotten what it once was, how ridiculous and frump-ish she had been. Forgotten, too, that her transformation in this respect she owed to Inez.

One summer afternoon and Nella was standing in front of Blossom's department store, gazing at the model in the window. The darkest grey, pinstriped, sleekly tailored suit, luxurious cream silk blouse; high-heeled patent court shoes.

Grandmother Georgina, from the earliest stage, had shaped Nella's fashion sense, dictated her appearance and would countenance no deviation. *You're short – the girlish type.* So Nella wore fussy dresses with puffed sleeves, abundant bows and frills; strappy shoes, coats of garish plaid; had her hair done in sausage curls. If ever it was necessary for her to wear a hat, it had a veil with velvet dots. She made the occasional, feeble move towards individual preference . . . *Well, if you think you can get away with something sophisticated, don't let me stop you making yourself ridiculous.* The battle, the humiliation, the continuous taunting made her so miserable she never dared to wear the offending items more than once.

But there, in Blossom's window, was the image of herself she had always secretly nurtured.

'Why not?' A pleasant, positive voice beside her. Inez. Nodding to the window. 'Nella, why not?'

'Um, well, no . . . Grandmother Georgina always –'

'For Christ's sake, Nella. She's been dead for months.'

Yes. But her spite went on haunting this poor woman in her late forties, her ludicrous dressiness: short, squat, a Shirley Temple look-alike. For God's sake, can anyone remember who *she* was?

'Come on, seek, there's a good dog.' And ushering the faintly murmuring Nella, Inez had them in the lift to

Ladies' Fashions before Nella could find a good reason to protest.

The trying-on session was lengthy. Nella, giddy with a sense of freedom, listening carefully to advice from Inez, from the store assistant, gazed, entranced, at constantly changing versions of herself. Eventually, Inez yawned and said, 'Nella, I have a hair appointment, upstairs. In five minutes.'

Nella received this inattentively.

'You can have it. Honestly, you've got pretty hair but . . . er . . .' The bobbing rolls of curls, sagging, unravelling. 'Come on.'

It was true, Nella's hair was silky and fine, a rich chestnut with the gentlest wave. After it had been shampooed, cut, sculpted into shape, Nella gazed, wide-eyed, not knowing herself.

'Super,' Inez said. 'Now let's have something to eat, I'm starving.'

High tea at Blossom's meant grilled gammon and egg, sauté potatoes, peas, wafer thin bread and butter. Caramel cheesecake to follow. When friends came up to the table, they said with genuine surprise, 'Nella – I'm sorry, I didn't recognise you.'

Nella preened, glowing with a faintly superior look of bewilderment. *What is all the fuss about?* Because this, after all, was her true self, compliments were her due. If it had anything to do with Inez, she managed, in a remarkably short space of time, to put it from her mind.

On this occasion, she insisted on paying the bill – 'My treat, I so seldom get the chance to shop with a friend. I'm so busy these days.'

Inez found this infinitely pathetic – when had Nella ever shopped with friends? She expressed her thanks, helped carry parcels to the car park. Nella eyed her Citroën 2CV. 'You know, Inez, Grandmother insisted I buy one of those. She said it gave me a young, dashing image.'

Inez could think of nothing to say except, 'Er . . .'

'But I'll tell you what. I've always hated it. What do you think about . . .'

She's got the bit between her teeth now, Inez thought. Good for her.

Chapter Five

Although Nella was late for the Friends of Clerehaven meeting she was in her seat when the evening began. Jaynie did not arrive until half-way through the slide talk, 'Rediscovering the gardens of Clerehaven's Manor House'. She caused maximum disruption, and so stunned the speaker with her smiling apology he forgave her instantly.

When the talk was over, questions asked and answered, during which Jaynie was fidgeting to boiling point, she was free to launch herself on the chairman, Evelina Barber.

Evelina, a delicate, graceful woman whose silvery voice and perfect diction proclaimed her years as a drama teacher, was most affectionately regarded by everyone; Inez and Dora were her particular friends.

Jaynie descended, brandishing the large folder she called her research which caused groans and occasional panic in everyone. She said to Evelina, 'Look, I've got this photograph. You remember it?'

Inez whispered to Dora, 'Hallo, Evelina, how are you? *Such* an interesting meeting . . .'

Evelina, bemused as the photograph was thrust beneath her face, fished for her spectacles. 'Well, I –'

'It was in your *garden*, you can't have *forgotten*.'

'Er . . .' Evelina said, looking for her place in a time long past.

'It was that garden party you gave for the Marie Curie foundation – *and* it happened to be your mother's eightieth birthday, too, so the party was for her, as well. Then she died a couple of weeks later, so I don't see how you can have *forgotten.*'

The photograph was of a mixed group in summer clothes, at least twenty people. As far as Jaynie was concerned there was only one: herself, as a teenager. 'I had a fringe then, well, just a short one. See. It suited me because of my cheekbones. I never had puppy fat like other teenagers. But I grew it out just after that and combed my hair straight back. Aah –'

Nella had so far managed to avoid Jaynie; incautiously, she passed too close. Jaynie's hand – ornate rings, clashing bangles – snaked out, fastened on her wrist. 'See, Nella, I bet you haven't forgotten, that's us at Evelina's garden party when we were youngsters together. See, you're near the end of that row.'

'I'm not,' Nella said, refusing to look, shaking her hand free. 'I wasn't there.'

Jaynie's laughter shrilled. 'Of course you were – no one could mistake that bright pink dress with the frills. My mother used to say it was called spearmint pink in Lancashire – you know, they used to have those Whit week walks, something religious, and all the mill workers wore new clothes and they wore either Whit week blue or spearmint pink. And – see – your face was *exactly* the same bright pink because you'd had too much sun and then afterwards you felt ill and Daddy drove you home . . .'

Inez and Dora exchanged signals: *This is too awful. What can we do?*

' . . . and there's Victor, your young brother, Evelina. Well, was. Did something that killed him, gliding, or falling out of an aeroplane or something . . .'

The only way Inez could have expressed her outrage would be to shout, 'This woman is bloody unbelievable.' It would scarcely help the situation.

'Oh, gosh, now *I've* forgotten. What was it?' Jaynie worried, frowning prettily.

33

On an automatic reflex, in a scarcely audible voice, Evelina said, 'A ballooning accident . . .'

'Yes. Well, there you are, people do these dangerous things – I'll never know why. Oh, God, he was good-looking, wasn't he? All the girls after him, but he always said he was going to marry me when I grew up. Do you remember, Evelina? *I'm your cavalier* he used to say to me – made me *promise* to marry him when I was old enough –'

Inez and Dora, giving up on the idea of stopping the unstoppable, resorted to diversionary tactics. Clear, carrying voices: 'Evelina, that business about altering the constitution –'

'If we don't have our arguments lined up for the AGM –'

'There's going to be the most awful debacle.'

'What, what?' Evelina said, flanked by two solid bodies, firm hands beneath her elbows. 'Dora . . . Inez . . . what?'

'We are removing you, physically, from that bloody woman,' Inez said out of the side of her mouth. 'Now, come on, before Dora handbags her.'

Later, they walked together, the three of them, through the mild night to Evelina's Victorian house in The Crescent; like Evelina, it was outdated, gracious, welcoming. 'What we all need,' Evelina said, ushering them into the drawing-room, 'is a jolly large drink.'

'What a civilised suggestion,' Inez agreed.

Evelina made for the drinks tray, murmuring, agonised, 'Jaynie Turner. Why in heaven's name did she have to come and live *here*?'

Dora volunteered, 'To find herself, she said.'

Inez gave a muffled, mad shriek.

And during the next hour, as they gossiped, who was it said, 'With any luck someone will murder the blasted woman'?

*   *   *

At mid-morning of the following day, Nella collected her post. She was beautifully turned out and, as she was expecting visitors, so was the house. Polished, tidy, flower-filled; a simple, tasty buffet lunch ready prepared by the submissive daily lady who found Nella a reasonable, if forbidding employer.

Nella took the post, and a cup of coffee, and sat before the fire in the sitting-room. She had worked through her guilt at defying Grandmother with surprising speed. Now she was free to enjoy making her everyday life pleasant, easy, even attractive, in direct defiance of Grandmother's belief that there was some positive moral value in being uncomfortable. Nella tried hard, but the central heating was antiquated and with a house of such a size, the work of renewing it seemed exorbitant. It never seemed to warm up, even at the height of summer; to counteract this, Nella indulged herself in baronial log fires that would have brought down on her all the rage of Grandmother's parsimony.

Sorting through the mail, she all at once sat rock-still, regarding the postmark and address on a typewritten, grubby envelope. After a while she stood up, paced the sitting-room in silent agitation, eventually – with a rush of anger – snatched up the envelope and opened it. There was no greeting, no signature. Just a typewritten sheet of paper. She read it several times, sat down suddenly and remained staring down at it, clutched crumpled in her podgy, manicured hand. After a while she roused herself.

In accordance with the final sentence she destroyed the letter by putting it in the fire, watched it burn; then she went away and busied herself as was necessary. It was some time before she returned, composedly poured herself a drink, looked round the room – assuring herself of its solidity, its permanence. She had devised this fortress for herself, nothing could assail her.

She spoke out loud, petulantly, 'Well, it's nothing to do with me. There's nothing I can do.'

Chapter Six

Midday, Friday, Inez sat at a table at the Cosa Nostra Bistro. She was to meet June – her friend from Byehaven – for lunch. June had sent a message to say she was delayed. As she was always delayed, Inez had brought a book and, with a glass of wine, settled herself contentedly to wait.

Distracted by a tapping sound she glanced up and, on a lightning reflex, away again.

Jaynie, exquisite, immaculate, was peering through the window, shielding her eyes to see through, and rapping on the glass.

Why can't the silly cow just open the door and walk in . . .?
Oh God, that's the last thing I want.

A waft of exotic scent, a perfectly made-up, perfectly featured face. Jaynie took a seat opposite Inez, ordered coffee and launched into her idea for the Clerehaven Summer Festival. A fashion parade – what else?

'. . . and we could all take part. Well, not *all*, not everyone's the right shape. But I'll make a pretty good showing on the catwalk . . . And I've already spoken to Marguerite Dean, you know, she's got Attitudes – just about the only decent boutique in town – I bought this from there last week . . .'

Of course you did. Since you came to live in Clerehaven Marguerite's paid off her mortgage.

'. . . I'm to phone tomorrow to fix up a meeting to discuss practicalities. She's very keen on the idea. Now, you must help, Inez.'

'You want me to be the strapping one in Sensible Clothes.'

'What? No, you never wear anything sensible. You'll have to be on the organising side. Well, you're – you're arty, you can see to the production.'

'Ah.'

Jaynie had more to say on the subject. Inez stopped listening and wondered if Jaynie would notice if she returned to her book.

'*Inez* – I said you and Dora Hope can liaise.'

'Right.'

'You can co-ordinate operations.'

'We can.'

'Yes.' Jaynie expounded – principally on what she would wear and what she would look like. Inez sank into a stupor, roused, an uncounted time later, to register Jaynie was saying something about an assignment. There was a telescoping of comprehension: key words *assignment* . . . *liaise* . . . *operations* strung themselves together in her mind.

'Good God, you're going to cover the war in Bosnia.'

Jaynie responded with a pained expression. 'Inez, half the time I don't know what you're talking about. No, I'm having my hair done this afternoon –'

'Yes, well, I suppose that is an essential preliminary,' Inez murmured.

'I always believe in looking my best when I'm pursuing my research, it's more professional . . .'

Inez's eyes were fastened on the door for the first glimpse of the late-arriving June. She had decided on her course of action.

'. . . although men never *expect* women to be professional, just feminine and silly and pretty. And, after all, the first stage of a relationship can be pretty tricky – although it's a long time since . . .'

June opened the door, saw the unmistakable back view of Jaynie and made a desperate face. Inez leapt up

– 'June, thank goodness, we'll miss our train . . .' – made a whirlwind exit, grabbing her coat from the stand and dragging June with her. 'I can't stand it, I can't stand it . . .' – pulling her coat on against the bitter wind.

Keeping pace, June said, 'We'll go to Emilio's. You don't think she'll follow us?'

'God, no, she's got to pay for her coffee, I'd paid for my wine. Anyway, if she does I'll empty a jug over her.'

On Monday evenings, old Mrs Hanks went to bingo and Inez took charge of the armadillo. A leisurely walk, cherished by both because it had the legitimacy of exercise and fresh air and invariably led to Inez's favourite pub, the One-eyed Rat. This was in one of the side streets that led down to the river, a not-much-visited part of town; unassuming, changing little over the years. The swinging sign showed a rat with an eye-patch and wearing a striped jersey dancing the hornpipe. A friendly notice in the window informed passers-by, 'You are welcome to bring your sandwiches at lunchtime.'

So many of the pubs in the more popular parts of Clerehaven were undergoing make-overs and emerging with 1930s decor and changed names – the latest the Toddies' Den. In the One-eyed Rat, there was an open fire, brass gleamed, oak settles lined the walls; its enduring ordinariness was a delight to those who knew it. 'But they're going down like nine-pins all over town. I'm holding out,' the landlord said to Inez.

'Stout fella.' Inez took her bottle of wine and a glass to a settle beside the fire.

The landlord leaned over the counter and looked down on the armadillo's bright, uplifted face. 'I'm warning you – any more getting into fights and singing filthy songs and you're out. For good. Oh . . . All right.' He pitched a packet of Things in a crackly bag over the counter. The armadillo caught it expertly, scuttled under

Inez's settle and began the systematic destruction of the bag and consumption of its contents.

Early evening, winter, the pub was quiet. There was no piped music, no juke box, but always magazines and newspapers about. Inez chose one and sat reading peacefully for a while; then her friend Dora came in. She took a glass from the bar, bought a packet of Things and, sitting down beside Inez, put it carefully on the floor. It disappeared at once. 'Hallo,' Dora said to underneath the settle. Tearing sounds answered her.

Inez poured wine into Dora's glass and they settled to a gossip.

Dora led the generous and gracious kind of life usually described as exemplary: charities, church work, school governorship, civic responsibility. Her husband, diffident and charming, considered – immovably – that civilisation depended on the values and lifestyle of people like themselves and trusted her implicitly to uphold them. Inez suspected it had never occurred to him that inside this dearly loved wife, mother, grand-mother, there lurked a rebel, never finding an outlet, expressing itself in quirky humour, subversion, and drinking in the One-eyed Rat with Inez.

Dora asked, 'Have you come across Jaynie lately?'

'Come across? What are you talking about? Don't we all hide in shop doorways?'

'Oh, all right. When did you last see her? Oblige me by thinking, you idiotic serving wench.'

'Well, um . . . Friday lunchtime. The Cosa Nostra. I was waiting for June, who was late, and Jaynie gate-crashed.'

Dora said nothing and looked thoughtful.

Inez said, 'Oh, please, she's disappeared. Someone's locked her in a cupboard to give us all a bit of peace. Dear Evelina's done her in and buried her under the floorboards.'

'It'd serve her right, she behaved with appalling insensitivity at the Friends' meeting.'

'So what's new?'

'But, Index, this is serious. The way I work it out, no one's seen her for three days.'

'*Three* . . .' Inez took this in. 'Three. Jaynie can't stay invisible for five minutes, never mind three days – *and* over a weekend. I didn't realise. Does anybody – I mean, have you asked . . .' she floundered.

'Yes. Tactfully as poss. Well, we're all being so tactful we're practically strangulated.'

'All?'

'The Camerons invited her to their drinks party Saturday lunchtime –'

'Pitifully misguided creatures.'

'Yes. Well, she simply didn't turn up, and not one word from her afterwards which, for all her faults, is not like Jaynie. She wasn't at church on Sunday –'

'Do you think God's decided he doesn't like her?'

'Pull yourself together, Index. This is becoming difficult and embarrassing. I don't want to poke my nose in, but in the event of *nobody* doing anything, I have a proposal.'

'Oh, golly yes.' Inez, feckless and irresponsible, was confident that whatever Dora suggested would be the right thing.

'So far, the latest I've managed to discover is – well, you saw her Friday lunchtime, but Friday *evening* – early evening – her neighbour across the road –'

'The one with all the poodles?'

'Yes. She saw Jaynie driving away. Since then, she did rather wonder at not seeing her about, so yesterday she went up the path and saw milk bottles not taken in, mail hanging out of the letter box. Now, Index, in view of that, we must ask around.'

'Oh, God, must we?' Inez groaned.

'Yes. It's the decent thing to do. Supposing she's had an accident or . . .' She studied her friend's face. 'What is it?'

'Well . . .' Inez thought back to the mind-stunning

interlude at the Cosa Nostra. 'I'm sorry, it's difficult to remember, I was just on autopilot – but she hinted about a date – or a meeting – or something. With a man.'

Dora looked bemused. 'A man?'

'Yes, dear. They're the ones with dicks.'

'But Jaynie's dead set against men – ever since Arthur left her. It's true there are plenty of chaps interested in her because of her looks, but she hasn't . . . She's never . . . Are you trying to tell me she's having an affair?'

'What I'm trying to tell you, Door, is that I wasn't listening to the bloody woman. All I did was register that she was being arch and secretive and congratulating herself about *something* – I don't know.'

'Think, dear girl, this could put a different complexion on things.'

Inez thought, unavailingly. 'An assignation – or an assignment.'

'Definitely those words?'

'Um, no. One of them. Or something. Door, why does this put a different thingy on things?'

'Well, just supposing she's gone off for a few illicit – or even licit – days with some chap? The last thing she'd want is us asking questions all over the place.'

'Do you think she has?'

Dora, sensible, intelligent, considered. 'No. And I don't know why. Well . . . if her absence was planned she would have given her apologies to the Camerons. Wouldn't she?'

'Not if she was in the grip of a hopelessly consuming passion. She could have flung caution to the . . .' Inez faltered to a stop beneath Dora's resigned stare.

'You've been reading the slosh page in women's mags again, haven't you? Look, I do think we must try to find out something, clarify the situation – but in view of what we know, or don't know, this calls for kid gloves. Bear that in mind, Watson. Tact.'

'Oh, God, yes, Holmes. Ratiocinate discreetly all over the place.'

Chapter Seven

Dora was the first to leave the One-eyed Rat. Inez stayed on, had a drink with friends then, at closing time, took the armadillo home. Her route took her down The Avenue, a winding road of disparate architectural styles, the older houses now smartened and restored, the new ones – like Jaynie's expansive bungalow – showy in weedless gardens. The armadillo came upon a driveway so deeply interesting Inez had to go after him. 'Oh, come on, old chap. You're always noseying about something.'

A light flickered on, off, at the perimeter of her vision; followed by a sound – a gate closing. It never occurred to her to examine this evidence of her senses until she had hauled the armadillo on to the pavement. Then she saw Nella – who could only have emerged from Jaynie's bungalow – walking briskly away into the misty darkness.

Her instantaneous reaction was: Well, there we are, all a storm in a teacup. I must tell Dora. Jaynie's home, Nella's just visited her –

And then the astonished backlash: When did Nella *ever* visit Jaynie?

The figure trotted busily round the corner, passed from sight. Inez strolled along the wall and high hedge of Jaynie's front garden until she came to the wrought-iron gates; they were shut. Standing close to them – having a slantwise view through the bushes that lined the drive – Inez could not make out any glimmer of light from the bungalow. It was hardly the thing to do, knock on the door at this hour . . . 'Oh, there you are, Jaynie. Good show. Door and I thought someone had kidnapped you.'

No.

She stood indecisively, then leaned down and clipped the armadillo's lead on. 'It'll do tomorrow, won't it?' She glanced towards the bungalow then down at the pointed muzzle, lifted interestedly to her. 'Well, it could have been worse. It could have been a man in a black mask with a bag marked Swag.'

She could hardly telephone Dora because her cantankerous mother-in-law – towards whom Dora behaved with saintly patience – grumbled furiously about calls after nine. The morning, then.

But the morning brought a collapse of Inez's tottering car battery (she must, must buy a new one). She had an early class and – having borrowed jump leads from her neighbour and arrived at college in roughly the same style as Batman – entirely forgot about speaking to Dora. When she remembered, in the evening, she also remembered that Dora was doing a one-day perambulation around relatives with her mother-in-law so that the old lady could make a complete nuisance of herself in households other than Dora's.

Next morning was market day, always a joy to Inez: the stalls, crammed together, long outspilling the medieval square, but still the bustle, the bargains, the gossip. Friends gathered, met for coffee; Inez found herself next to Nella in the lace-tableclothed Spider's Web tearooms.

Inez said, without thought, 'Well, now we know Jaynie's back.'

Nella stared at her, stony-faced, said expressionlessly,

'What? Who?' As if she had never heard the name before.

Inez remembered, too late. The Row. Everyone went to such polite lengths to overlook it, and Nella and Jaynie managed a kind of social interaction where it never surfaced, so that Inez was not the only one to forget it had ever happened. She found herself incoherent. 'Well, but she was – no one's seen – everyone wondered – and, Monday night – her house – I thought . . .'

Nella continued to stare at her. Inez clamped her mouth shut, determined not to be provoked. But Nella inclined towards her, diction of sawmill penetration; there was, for an instant, a terrifying reprise of Grandmother Georgina. 'I have no idea what you are talking about, Inez.'

She turned away with a smile so superior Inez's reaction was spontaneous. 'Oh, haven't you? Then it wasn't you calling on her on Monday evening?'

'*Calling?* On . . .' Nella left the name unspoken. True Lynchet tactic; they ordered the universe to suit themselves; if they wished not to know someone, ergo, the unfortunate bugger didn't exist.

But it was not like Nella to be so unsubtle; personal animosity, out in the open, embarrassed everyone – and made Nella vulnerable. Perhaps Nella was growing more into her grandmother's role, perhaps her career as Alfred's surrogate was sending her a little out of balance.

Nella stared somewhere beyond Inez. 'It's terribly bad form to go around repeating gossip. But still, everyone knows you arty and unreliable types go in for hallucinations.'

'I don't . . .' Inez began, but Nella had turned away and begun a conversation with someone else.

The morning of the following day Dora telephoned. Inez

said, 'I remembered Jaynie said something about Marguerite Dean – you know, she's the boutique. So I called in there yesterday, had a tactful word.'

'Had she seen her?'

'No, Jaynie was supposed to telephone her, but she didn't. She is a bit scatterbrained anway, so Marguerite didn't think much about it.'

'Mmm. No joy with me, either. And it's five days.'

What could she say, about Nella coming out of Jaynie's gate, about Nella's screamingly obvious dishonest reaction? Some instinct she could not name made her swallow this information; dissemble – to her dear, dear friend. Thank God they weren't face to face: one look and Dora would know she was hiding something. It was that appalling Jaynie brought you to such straits. 'Um, Door, have you thought of asking Nella . . .?'

'Darling, have you got softening of the brain? *Nella*. Nella wouldn't care if no one set eyes on Jaynie ever again.'

True enough. 'Door, how could anyone mislay Jaynie?'

'Exactly.'

'So what do we . . .?'

'I'll phone Arthur, it's the only thing I can think of. I'll get back to you.'

When she did it was to report that Arthur was away, with his new wife, walking in the Lakes – 'His secretary doesn't know precisely where, and none of the other staff will. All they know is he's due back in two days.'

'That'll make it . . . if she doesn't . . .'

'Yes. Index, I've got a nasty feeling about this.'

'Me, too. Are we being fanciful? This middle-class diffidence about interfering in people's private affairs . . .'

'Yes. But we must be practical, and Christian. Who knows where she is or what has . . . Well, we can't contact Arthur. I'd try her children but I don't know where to find them. I don't even know their names. Do you?'

'Er . . . Tom and Maggie Tulliver.'

'Oh, God, I can always rely on you to be ridiculous,' Dora said wearily. 'There's only one thing now. So who contacts the police?'

After a small silence, Inez said, 'Door, that's – er – pretty extreme.'

'Yes. But I think it's something we should do.'

'You. You have gravitas.'

'I've got a tight schedule, too. Oh, all right.'

Chapter Eight

It was called an inner city area, although any association with the lives of people busying themselves, deriving meaning from productiveness, from industry, from the worth of everyday achievement, had long since disappeared.

Blighted, broken down: empty warehouses, abandoned factories, deserted workshops. Heaving concrete, mangled wire fencing, graffiti too tired now to proclaim anything except hopelessness – and in amongst this detritus, this scarred and violent dereliction, suddenly, amazingly: a pale blue BMW 325.

As it was late, and dark, no one was about to see who had abandoned it; the meths drinkers and bag people had the comfort of company and the warmth of their fire over half a mile away, closer to the sleepless housing estate, where at least there were humanity and voices, and the perambulating soup and buns of the caring.

The BMW was less than a year old, in perfect condition and full working order; such good fortune had never before visited this destroyed landscape.

By the next morning the osmosis that operates in desperate areas ensured that within hours every part of it that could be turned to profit had been removed: tax disc, battery, number plates, radio, windscreen wipers, wheels; petrol siphoned from the tank.

After it had been stripped down to a shell, it was the turn of the kids who, eventually, tired of ripping and smashing and wrenching, set fire to it.

During the night a storm broke, a roaring wind, drenching downpours of rain. The rain continued most of the next day, until every evidence of ownership of the car – incinerated, vandalised – was washed away.

The only immovable identification, the chassis number, stamped into the metalwork, could not be obliterated except by filing, and there was no one sophisticated enough to do that, or even see any reason to.

The area known as Hasley Bridge stood on the western edge of Chatfield. Although it had the melancholy, dilapidated aspect of a place fallen upon hard times, vandalism had not overwhelmed it. There were enclaves of respectability: cramped terraces, grimy but cared-for, with donkey-stoned steps, sparkling white net curtains; a small sixties development, all matchboard, straight lines and struggling gardens; the occasional huddle of pre-war semis, bay windows, pretty front doors with stained glass ovals. It was the once grand merchants' houses that suffered most. As late as the 1950s they were in single occupancy – the front door opened by an aproned maid; tradesmen side door only; a gardener at work amongst the rose arbours and rockeries. Forty years on, they were abandoned to the creeping decay of bedsits and single rooms, DSS bed and breakfast; proud carriageways crammed with every variety of vehicle from a broken perambulator to a rust-eaten Ford Escort, the shaven lawns and raked drives no more than a memory.

The grandest of these, Old Park House, was completely derelict, a skeleton bounded by vanished securities – the double gates destroyed, the garden walls a tumble of broken brick and twisted, slender railings, grounds litter-strewn, rampantly overgrown.

But just as some urban deity kept Hasley Bridge from complete decline so local superstition kept people away from Old Park House. Although not entirely. Those who knew used it as a hiding place for their various concerns, the roofless rooms still providing corners for concealment, odd recesses for privacy and shelter.

Every Wednesday evening that was exactly what the couple went in search of. They were local, they knew how to approach, separately, seeking out the darkened areas between the street lights, the shelter of massive shrubs and old trees; turning abruptly into the narrow track (when it was originally laid down, wide enough only for a cart). A few quick paces along and they could slip into the side of the house – wait in the remains of an elegant side porch – meet, clasp, pant, grope.

There were few words, their adulterous affair was flaring, dangerous, and discovery would make their lives unendurable – which they pretty much approached now – but here, in the winter, out of the everyday, they could lose themselves in an hour of uninhibited rutting. That was how he might have expressed it, had he dared tell anyone. For her the buried longing for romance stayed buried; she was forty-five, the mother of three, not much came her way – which made her philosophically inclined to accept whatever was on offer.

The upstairs of Old Park House was much too dangerous to venture into, their territory was the still stout-walled and partially roofed old butler's pantry which they found ideally met their requirements. The woman, ever practical, had a folded plastic sheet in her large handbag – but that night saw a dreadful curtailment in its use.

There was the smell first. They were accustomed to smells of every strength and offensiveness which they were able to ignore not by an act of will so much as by the deodorising reflex of sexual arousal. But this barrier – cloying, sickly – they penetrated too abruptly, then reeled from the full impact of its stench, held aghast by a havoc of images: the prone figure, tangle of gold hair,

49

blue, swollen lips, maggot-seething flesh . . . The defenceless, outflung arm. The slender white hand clenched to a fist.

They fled, stood in the litter-strewn passageway, stared at each other, speechless. At last she whispered, 'She's dead – she's dead.'

'Course she is.' His voice was low, terrified, furious.

'We'll have to – tell – someone –'

'Tell? Tell who, you stupid cow? We *tell* someone and we'll have to say what we was doing here. You going to take that on board – no, you're bloody not. 'Sides, we'd be implicated – suspects. I'm having nowt to do with the filth. So keep your mouth shut. D'you hear that – *keep your fucking mouth shut*. C'mon.' He blundered off, not waiting for her, not looking back.

She spent a sleepless night, every time she closed her eyes images fractured and re-formed: slender body, bright hair tousled in a shaft of moonlight, elegant shoes, rotting flesh. She woke with a headache, distracted (although no one in her family was interested enough to notice), haunted by the fate of the woman – dreadful enough – but how much more horrifying to lie alone and abandoned in that broken-down, lonely place . . .

By lunchtime, when she finished her stint at Norton Packaging, she had made up her mind. Daring, heart thumping, knowing she would never confess this to him (if she ever saw him again), she set out walking briskly across Chatfield.

It took her fifteen minutes to the centre of town; her destination was the railway station, its row of telephone boxes. She had seen people do it on telly – put a handkerchief over the mouthpiece of the receiver.

She was so nervous her voice came out breathy and rushed. 'Hasley Bridge. Old Park House. The body of a woman. Last night.'

'Who is –?'

Before the sentence was completed she had crashed down the receiver and was scurrying away.

At once a mobile was despatched from the control office at Chatfield subdivisional headquarters with instructions to establish whether they did have a body. Or was it a hoax?

They had a body. Old Park House was now a crime scene.

Detective Chief Inspector Sheldon Hunter, tied up giving evidence at Chatfield Crown Court all day, pawed the ground and reflected there was nothing so maddening as being bleeped and helpless to respond. Freed at last, he raced to Hasley. Old Park House could be nothing but a melancholy site. The violent storm of the previous Friday, rumbling on for two days, had worked its havoc through the half roofless house: the rubble-strewn ground covered a deep litter of autumn leaves, soaked and mashed, yielding – he was immediately given to understand – nothing in the way of footprints.

The unit had been hard at work, the body removed and delivered to the mortuary in Chatfield while an exhaustive search continued. What he learnt immediately was that she had been strangled with a silk scarf – most probably her own. There were no marks on her hands – beautifully shaped hands, soft, manicured, the enamelled nails unbroken. It would appear, then, that she had not attempted to defend herself, which seemed scarcely believable. There was no handbag in the vicinity, no pockets in her clothes to give any clue to her identity.

Hunter shrugged himself into his British warm. There was much for him to consider and there was also something beyond immediate necessity . . . a nudge. Intuition. Memory. Memory? He paused in that despairing place. But no. Whatever it was, prowling through the past, he could not retrieve it.

Hunter sat in his office at Chatfield subdivisional head-quarters. Six foot three, built outwards to match; a strong, clever face, wary and compassionate, eyes as grey as a winter sea. His size, his personality, dominated whatever company he found himself in – this was not something he set out deliberately to do, simply that his presence always had to be taken account of. Particularly by his troops, who were so confounded by his unintentional non sequiturs that they frequently had the vertiginous sense of falling into his mind.

He had read the reports of the investigating officer and the duty forensic pathologist, discussed them with the duty sergeant Tom Hopper and was on the point of winding up this stage of the proceedings.

'Nothing's come up about the phone call?' Hopper said.

'No.' And they knew nothing was likely to. Chatfield was not yet equipped with the facility to trace calls made direct to its number. If the caller – assumed to be female although her voice had been deliberately muffled – had dialled 999 the call would have been automatically recorded.

Preliminary enquiries had begun in the immediate locality, so far without the least hint that anyone had set eyes on the unknown woman. It was impossible to believe that anyone who had seen her anywhere near Hasley could have failed to notice her, to turn and stare – with curiosity, lust or longing – at the beautifully dressed, slender, blonde woman. Therefore it was to be presumed she had been taken there after her death; the indisputable pattern of lividity – of blood settling by gravity when her circulation ceased – proved that she

had been murdered in a sitting position, and then trans-
ported to Old Park House.

There, she had been laid out in a seemly way, not
raped, not mutilated, not robbed, she still wore her
watch, bracelet, necklace, all expensive items. Her jew-
ellery, her clothes, would help to identify her – but it
would not be long before someone claimed her. She was
a woman of background, status – not a vagrant, a drifter,
a ship passing in the night.

It was generally understood there could be any number of reasons why she had not been reported missing
although it was estimated her body had been lying in
Old Park House for approximately five days. It might
have been known to her friends and relatives that she
was on holiday, on a business trip, had matters of her
own to attend to and would not return until a specified
date. Assuming she had friends and relatives who
would notice her absence.

The answer was not long delayed. The incident room
had been set up, HOLMES moved in overnight. Detective Sergeant James Collier – lately returned from a
computer course and talking, in Hunter's opinion, like a
Dalek – could not entirely conceal his satisfaction at
presenting Hunter with a print-out from the PNC
wanted/missing persons index. It was, to Sergeant
Hopper's jaundiced eye, reminiscent of a puppy bringing a bone to its master

DS Collier had never made a secret of being gay and
in consequence had to contend with every attitude from
indifference to the most vicious homophobia. It never
occurred to him to give up and do something else, he
was young enough to keep fighting for a place in the
career he valued above everything. He had never been
asked by Hunter to account for his gender preference;
Hunter, who knew Collier's qualities, was well known
not to care whether anyone was male, female, both or
neither – so long as they were good at the job.

According to the print-out, Mrs Dora Hope, of Ash-

53

dene, High Town, Clerehaven had gone into Clerehaven police station on the previous day, Thursday. She was concerned about a neighbour who had not been seen since Friday, midday, 29th October. The neighbour, Mrs Jaynie Turner, was fifty years old, five foot six, slim, blonde. Her address: 14 The Avenue, Clerehaven.

'It's her,' Collier said. 'It's got to be, hasn't it, guv?'

'And Clerehaven's twenty miles away. So what was she doing in Chatfield?' Hunter asked.

Chapter Nine

It was the first frost of winter, crunchy, tinsel sparkling. Clerehaven lay, shrouded and ghostly, clenched into freezing cold, thick ground fog.

A uniformed constable stood guard in the driveway of 14 The Avenue behind the wrought-iron double gates. In the road a scattering of onlookers lingered with idle interest and, distinguished by their ferociously concentrated attention, the media – cameras, ENGs, microphones – foregathered in the assumption that as a beautiful woman had met a violent death, *everyone* would want to know why, how, whoever. 'Mr Hunter, can you tell us –?' 'Not at the moment,' Hunter said, surging unstoppably through them.

And then, stepping into the hall, pausing. This had been her home, the focus of her being, where she had lived her everyday life – and met her death? The most thorough forensic investigation was in progress, the scene-of-crime men working their way painstakingly through the bungalow, and it was already becoming evident that nothing untoward had occurred in this showy, obsessively cared-for place.

The bungalow was large, modern, furnished and decorated with an excess of luxurious show. In the sitting-room, every possible surface contained dolls: coiffed, frantically dressed in costumes from all corners of the world, all periods of questionable history. And photographs, countless ornately framed photographs of herself: one of her with two youngsters, from a faintly traceable likeness her children; several of her with a heavily handsome older man, presumably her father. None at all of her ex-husband.

And mirrors; large, small, elaborate, all arranged at a height he knew matched that of the dead woman, all endlessly reproducing the reassurance of her image, because – the notion occurring instantaneously – no matter how often, how many visitors sat in this room, the mirrors were not for them, her gaze would slide, unseeing, across their reflections, seeking always to come to rest on the reassurance of herself. Hunter sat quietly, thinking over the moment of intuition that had yielded up to him Jaynie Turner: pretty, ageless, self-absorbed, glowingly at the centre of her own universe . . . Was that why she had died?

A dainty lady's desk, reproduction antique, stood in the bay window looking on to a rear garden of geometric exactitude and every conceivable dinkiness in the way of garden ornament. In the thick crusting of frost it looked like Santa's grotto.

The desk was to him enviously neat, he had never known how to keep a desk tidy in the whole of his life. He sat down, began his patient examination.

The necessary documents were allotted to their own folders and drawers: household, finance, car, personal – everything essential and admirably ordered. There was a spiral notebook, many pages filled with childishly rounded, occasionally askew handwriting he had no doubt was hers. The first two pages contained a list of books all relating to genealogy. On the following pages – headed by dates from the autumn of the previous year – were brief notes on the practice of genealogy and local history and then long passages which, by their style and content, were obviously copied from the books listed on the first page.

So . . . she had been attending a course on the subject and was clearly not at home with the written word – hence the brevity of the notes and the long copied extracts. He picked up a large, important loose-leaf file labelled 'Research'. Contents were listed on the first page and the file was made up of separate envelopes, each with a small tab for indexing, some filled in, some blank.

He skipped through the list:

local newspapers: photos, advertisements
local magazines   "   "
oral information – memories
Gen Reg Office, St Catherine's House.

There were several more; he glanced in the envelope for Gen Reg Office and found three handwritten pages headed: 'Details necessary to supply for getting' and then, variously, birth, marriage, death certificates. 'Details' was printed in capitals and underlined. There were a few copies of certificates with names that meant nothing to him.

He riffled through the other envelopes; their sequence had only an eccentric relation to the index. She obviously set great store by her 'research' but she was hopeless at it, incapable of organising her sources, her notes, or – he suspected – herself. He could not know why she had undertaken this project, except, perhaps, as some kind of distraction – the whole thing was a mess. It was when he came to the envelope in the file relating to herself that the explanation at once presented itself. The file was bulging, every certificate from birth, baptism, marriage, decree absolute. School reports, photographs, family tree – both sides of the family. He glanced through until his boredom reached crisis point, thrust everything back.

Replacing everything, he came upon a diary bound in pink taffeta. He opened it. The gold-bordered pages contained miniature coloured illustrations of sundials in gardens and thatched cottages; there was an uplifting sentiment for each week. *God gave us memories so that we*

might have roses in December . . . The layout was a week
per page. The double page spread for the previous week
showed a central heating service for the Monday afternoon, Tuesday blank, Thursday evening a meeting of
the Friends of Clerehaven Society. For Friday, the day
she went missing, 'S & S, Crowning Glory 4.30 p.m.';
this had been crossed through, the appointment
repeated for the next day, 10.15 a.m. Also on the Friday
the entry appeared: 'C. station 5.30. B.N.'

He considered it. Clerehaven station? He was too old
a hound to think it could be as simple as that, but it was
a start. He spent some time going carefully through the
rest of the desk, then called to DC Annette Jones,
recently moved to CID, working quietly and efficiently
through the bedrooms. 'You haven't come across an
address book, have you?'

'Not yet, guv. Wouldn't it be . . .?' Her gaze ranged
over the desk.

'Nope. But she could have taken it into another
room.'

'Well, yes,' she said doubtfully.

He looked a question. Their relationship was based on
mutual respect; he could not admit she was his
favourite, but he could acknowledge her intelligence
and intuition, had been known to claim she was the best
chap he had – just for the pleasure of seeing her sparkling response. That she was a raven-haired, gainly five
foot eight, with a curving, red-lipped smile, he allowed
to influence him completely. He was only human.

'It's just that, so far, there's not a speck of dust out of
place. She strikes me as a woman who obsessively
plumps cushions and polishes taps – if she took her
address book into another room, she'd make sure she
brought it back, put it there. Exactly. By the phone.'

He nodded. Slid the diary across, showed her the
Friday entry.

She said thoughtfully, 'C? Clerehaven? Or it could be

Chatfield, couldn't it? After all, that's where she was found.'

'Yes, but she was seen setting out in her car. She could have picked someone up from Clerehaven, then driven to Chatfield. So let's start locally. Have we got an exact time she was seen leaving here?'

'No. It's the woman across the road, she's pretty vague – except when it comes to poodles.'

'Poodles?'

'Yes, she's got a house full of them. She can only see the end of the drive from her window, but she did see Jaynie Turner pull out of the drive, close the gates, get back in her car and drive off.'

'Alone?'

'The thing is, guv, it was dark by then – well-lit enough on this road, but not enough to see inside a car.'

'Right. So, we start at Clerehaven station. You know what we want.'

'Was a train due in five thirty on that date? If yes – from where? Did anyone see, speak to, Jaynie Turner? Recognise her car?'

'Good. As for B.N., we keep him, her or it to ourselves for the present. Now, I'm going walkabout. I want to speak to Mrs Hope, the woman who reported her missing, see where that leads. Off you go then, improve the shining hour.'

It had already been established that Jaynie's cleaning lady would not be any help, she was on a two-month convalescence after surgery. Jaynie had not engaged anyone else, preferring to manage herself temporarily. Her garden – minutely examined for anything that might shed light on her last hours – had remarkably managed to take on the same stunned gaudiness as the bungalow. Strolling round it, Hunter registered, with disbelief, one garden gnome mooning, another flashing. He glanced towards the bungalow. From a window Annette made a mad face at him.

On his way out, he spoke to the house-to-house enquiry team leader, one of his Chatfield contingent, leaving instructions for a thorough trawl round the neighbours to find if anyone could pinpoint the time Jaynie was seen driving away. Then, after receiving directions from the control room, he set out for High Town.

Mrs Hope lived on one of the many unmade, tree-lined roads, in a gabled 1920s house set in a spreading garden. She regarded his badge thoughtfully, 'Do come in.'

A mature woman, statuesque, beautiful, a grand-mother (judging by the photographs scattered about her comfortable sitting-room), with a manner so charming and easy he experienced a momentary dislocation of the senses . . . *he was a valued friend, at home here, dropping by on some personal, some social matter* . . .

No. He was a plodding, hairy-arsed old copper going about his job.

She offered him coffee, which he refused; they sat down. She said, gravely and unflinchingly, 'This is the most dreadful thing, Mr Hunter, this violence in our community. One hears, one reads of such matters, but I can honestly say it's an experience I've never had, never dreamt of – the murder of someone known to me. We all feel helpless, shocked, and inadequate. Because, you see, much as I want to help, I really don't think there is anything I can say to you that will be of use.'

'Right. Shall I decide about that, Mrs Hope?'

'I'm sure you will.'

'You reported her missing. What made you do that?'

She could have answered *Because she was* but she was too intelligent to take the question as meaningless and there was nothing defensive or self-justifying in her manner. She explained, with admirable clarity, the Friends of Clerehaven meeting. ' . . . that being the last time I personally saw her. She was very much a social person, you see, and because she was so attractive, very – visible – people missed her. And over the weekend she didn't turn up at places where she was expected.'

'Such as?'

'Um, the Camerons, they'd invited her for lunchtime drinks on Saturday – a week ago – but she simply never appeared. Didn't phone to apologise or explain – that wasn't a bit like her. She was a reasonably regular churchgoer, and Saturday she was on the flower rota at St Botolph's, and *that* wasn't like her, to let everyone down, and when she didn't come to Sunday morning service . . . And then, well, you should speak to my friend, Mrs Inez Bryant, because she saw her – briefly – the day after the Friends meeting and . . .' she faltered, 'as far as we can make out, no one saw her after that.'

He paused, studied her. 'What made you hesitate, Mrs Hope?'

She looked apologetic and caught out. 'Well, it must seem very gossipy and prying – Inez and I trying to work out when we'd last seen her, where she could be. But it really wasn't like that. We were being as discreet as possible because Jaynie *could* have been about some blameless and private business and the last thing she'd want was everyone asking where she was. And I was concerned – Inez doesn't take much notice of what goes on around her but she agreed with me it was so much out of character . . .'

He let her talk on for a while; she was sincere in her good-natured concern, in her middle-class reluctance to mind anyone else's business. But in the reserve that echoed behind her words lay an unmeasured and resolute distance between herself and Jaynie Turner.

He considered it. When she referred to Mrs Bryant as her friend it was with the ease of long familiarity; she would find it difficult, impossible at this stage, to admit that she and her friend disliked Jaynie Turner. And it was not a question he would ask her. Not yet.

As she showed him out, she said, 'I did try to get in

61

touch with Arthur – her ex-husband – before I started any other enquiries, but –'

'Yes. He was away.'

'Poor man,' she murmured, heartfelt. 'Such a nice man . . .'

'Not much of a holiday homecoming for him. He had to identify her.'

'Oh, good gracious . . .'

They stood in the wide, beautifully tiled porch; the view of the frost-hung garden was exquisite. 'Mrs Hope, I understand. You didn't want to cause scandal, embarrassment for Mrs Turner, her family or friends. You did what you believed was right. And you *were* right.'

'Thank you, I think that makes me feel better. I did wrestle with my conscience before I went to the police. It seemed such an *extreme* action. I didn't do it lightly.'

'Of course not.' But she was the only one out of all the neighbours, friends, acquaintances who had done it at all. It would seem that Mrs Jaynie Turner was not a woman people cared about a great deal.

She asked him if he was going to see Mrs Bryant, and when he said yes she walked helpfully with him down the drive, 'Look, it's much better if you leave your car there, you'll find it easier to walk.' She gave him the address, directions, held out a firm hand to shake his. 'I do hope you can . . . you will . . . catch . . . discover . . . I mean . . . oh dear.' She turned and walked quickly back to her house.

From his car he telephoned Jaynie Turner's number and left a message for Annette to meet him at Mrs Bryant's house. Then he set out.

Chapter Ten

He had a recollection of a visit to Clerehaven, long ago, a family outing when his daughter was a little girl, spending the day as so many people did, in holiday mood, in the summer. But that Clerehaven had slipped into the past, unrecognisable now as this mist-hanging town of interweaving streets and stealing silence. He walked through it, hunched up in his British warm, following Mrs Hope's directions, losing his way, finding it again. Everything was intermingled: houses, gardens, shops, parks, businesses.

As he negotiated a flight of steps and a footpath, he could understand why she had advised him not to take his car, but . . . *easier to walk*? Was this some kind of local humour? Did this bloody Cremorne exist?

At last, almost walking past the recessed entrance, he found himself studying, in admiration, the high, splendidly carved gates. He went through them.

Anything called Cremorne, in this town, had to be potty. And beautiful. It took his breath away: the bare branches of a weeping willow frozen into a silver cascade; bushes shrouded in spiders' webs like white lace. He walked down curving gravelled paths enclosed by shrubberies glittering with scarlet berries and frost-edged gold leaves. And here and there, with their walls of softly worn old brick, weathered stone, the houses, hiding from each other.

So why should he be surprised to come upon two people, one of whom – a tall, eye-catching woman dressed in something flowing – was about to climb into a shopping trolley? She was accompanied by a young man, smart, slim as a whippet, with chestnut hair and wide blue eyes and the same scrubbed, head prefect look of Sergeant James Collier.

Inez gracefully abandoned her attempt to get into the trolley, a piece of foolery for herself and Sam, dismissed in the presence of strangers. Especially a stranger as big and beautiful as this. Good God . . .

It was the first time since Joe's death she had experienced any sensuous response to a man – who was looking with interest, not at her, but at the trolley.

She said, 'I say, it's not yours, is it? Have you come to collect it?' Then, registering his blank look, 'No, of course not. People just abandon the damn things here. You know, like an elephants' graveyard.'

Sam said, 'And it must be at least a mile and a half from its home.'

'So we were going to take it back, on our way. May I help you?'

Closer, Hunter could see a sprinkling of grey in her mop of tousled brown hair. She was his age, older perhaps, her face was serene, pleasing; a small nose, classically Greek, warm brown eyes; there was something bountiful about her that said she would laugh easily, forgive readily.

He said, 'I'm looking for Mrs Bryant. I understand she lives here.'

Something long-forgotten in Inez squeaked, *He's looking for me? I have this kind of luck . . .?*

She said, 'She does. I mean, I do. You've found her.'

He was producing some kind of official identification.

I refuse to believe he's come to read the gas meter . . .

'I'm Detective Chief Inspector Hunter of Chatfield subdivisional headquarters.'

Their immediate reaction – the swiftly exchanged

glance, the frivolity quenched – reminded him, inescapably, of well-mannered children caught out in a prank.

'It's about Jaynie Turner, isn't it?'

'Yes. If I could have just a little of your time.'

'Absolutely. Of course.'

Hunter's gaze was drawn irresistibly to the country-looking wicker basket which the young man placed in the trolley. It held a jam jar of something with a gingham cover, half a dozen dainty small cakes, wrapped in cellophane – and a large plate pie of golden pastry. His mother had made pies like that when he was a boy, crumbling, rich . . . Hunter could have fallen on it and wolfed it down.

Inez passed the trolley to Sam, 'Cut along now, there's a good chap. See you at the Market Hall.'

'Right-ho, mater.' He set off at a trundling gallop with great good humour.

'Your son?' Hunter enquired. He had heard more or less everything in the course of his life, but never anyone addressed as mater. He had already decided that in this eerie, vertiginous, make-believe place, anything could happen.

'My . . . Good God, no. I've never whelped,' Inez said mildly. 'He's my pal, Sam. It's the cancer research fund charity morning. We take things, and sell them, and buy them off each other.'

'Yours was the pie,' he said, studiedly neutral.

'Lamb and mint.' Her tone matched his. 'Sam's the fairy cakes. Now, let's go in, you could lose your knackers standing about in this cold.'

He could think of nothing at all to say.

Her house was of whitewashed stone, the doorway so low he had to stoop. In the hall he trod on York flagstones it had taken three hundred years to wear smooth. There was a console table of Mexican pine, on its lower shelf a pewter jug, turned on its side, from which copper beech leaves spilled. She led him through to the living-room. The windows were small, peering – but there were many of them, set at all levels, the winter light came in at many angles and different densities giving the room a soft, shifting glimmer.

There were only two photographs displayed on a splendid Welsh dresser. One of a thin woman with a plain face and gentle smile standing before the cottage, taken some past summer. Inez said, 'My cousin, Mary Weller, this was her house, she lived here all her life. She left it to me in her will, seven years ago, or can it be eight now?'

The other, larger photograph, noticeable because of its prominent position, showed a big, untidy, friendly-looking man, his arm about Inez's shoulders; they were smiling at one another.

'Your husband?' Hunter said.

'Yes.' There was a pause. 'He died the year before I came here.'

'Oh, I'm so . . . I . . .'

'No, it's all right.' But she touched the photograph, minutely rearranging it as if, simply by looking, he had somehow trespassed. Turned to him with a smile. 'I say, let's have some coffee, shall we?'

In the kitchen there was a small, beautifully restored iron range, open shelves crammed with domestic essentials, a sense of unfussed efficiency, the smell of mint and lemons; a generous kitchen table bore the signs of many uses. Inez sat Hunter down at it, put mugs, sugar and milk in front of him, switched on the kettle.

He said, 'I've been speaking to your friend, Mrs Hope. She told me that you saw Mrs Turner the day she went missing.'

Inez sat down opposite, looked directly at him. 'What's happened to her? It's the most appalling thing, none of us can quite grasp it. What was so awful, I never took it seriously – when Dora and I were discussing what to do – if we should do anything. Well, it's Dora who does things, she's the one with the Christian con- science. I just make unseemly jokes.'

'About what?'

She looked awkward, 'Oh, um, daft things.'

He waited, but she busied herself cutting him a slice of rich fruit cake. The coffee made, she sat down again; there was a suggestion of shoulders being squared, getting down to business.

He thought, someone else who hadn't liked Jaynie Turner.

'Do you know if she had any enemies?'

'No.' She shook her head vehemently. 'Not someone who would – good God, no.'

'She said nothing to you about someone behaving in a strange or threatening way to her?'

'No.'

'Would she have confided in you?'

'Confided?' She looked bemused, as if this was a thought too outlandish to be comprehended. 'No. Why should she?'

'You were her friend . . .' He paused deliberately. 'Weren't you?'

'Well, I knew her.'

'That isn't an answer.'

'No.' She looked out of the window: at the radiance of ice, the mystery of fog. Turned back to him after a long moment. 'I am genuinely deeply sorry that such a frightful thing has happened to her. But, I have to be honest – I didn't like her. Somehow that makes things worse.'

'You can't go back and turn her into someone you did like.'

'No, no I can't. So I'm stuck with it.'

'Yep.'

She smiled, but such a smile, a candid admission of a very human failing; he had to smile back. 'All right. Give in. But what can I tell you? I'm damned if I know.'

'What about the last time you saw her?'

She described her encounter with Jaynie in the bistro,

making no apology for not listening to her – except in so much as, if she had, she might have had something to contribute to his enquiries.

'Don't bother about it,' he said easily. 'She seemed very taken up with this local history project.'

'That was tosh. Sorry, but it was. She needed to get her life together after divorce – and for Jaynie that meant being the centre of attention. She did enjoy embarrassing people by digging up things they'd rather leave forgotten. Nothing important, just trivia . . .' She chatted for a while: names, occasions. He gave mild encouragement, mentally sorting and filing with shrewd precision.

'Do you think it could be something connected with her research that she was telling you about?'

'And I wasn't listening. Honestly, I don't know. You never knew what she was up to until she chose to tell. She would drop the odd hint, archly, then pretend it was nothing. She loved being secret.'

An inquisitive woman who delved into other people's affairs and then delightedly broadcast whatever she discovered. It was a fair bet that this time she hadn't been given the chance.

Chapter Eleven

They left Inez's house together and, walking along the paths between shrubs and lawns, were overtaken by a lanky, dishevelled man moving rapidly. He called a greeting as he passed to which Inez replied cheerfully, at the same time politely edging Hunter to one side, murmuring, 'Mind you don't get caught in his slipstream – whoops.' This as he executed a complicated galloping sidestep, narrowly avoiding Annette who was standing lost in admiration before the carved gates.

He had apologised and flung himself out into Clerehaven in a matter of seconds, while Annette was saying, 'Er . . .'

Hunter introduced Inez who said, 'Sorry, my neighbour.'

Annette gazed after the flying figure. 'Isn't he the chap on telly who does that series about the Middle Ages?'

'Yes, we learn to dodge when we hear him coming. He's probably forgotten something. He's always forgetting things. Rumour has it his wife left him because he could never remember her name. Well, jolly nice to meet you. Must find what Sam's done with that damned trolley, be just like him to shove it in his front garden and fill it with plants. Cheerio.' She went on her way, striding tall, faintly exotic, into the mist.

Annette smiled goodbye, puzzled. 'Sam? Trolley?'

'Oh, don't ask,' Hunter said. 'Now, I left my car at Mrs Hope's. She said it was easier to walk.'

'Ah,' Annette said thoughtfully. 'And was it?'

'Well . . .'

'Me, too. There's something distinctly spooky about this place, isn't there?'

'Nonsense,' Hunter said bracingly and then – after they had taken an unrecognisable turning into a huddled and charming lane, walked down a cobbled passageway and found themselves looking at the United Reform church – 'You can bloody say that again.' Setting out, determined: 'If we keep climbing, dammit, it's High Town, it's got to be up there somewhere. Right. Now. What?'

Annette told him. On the Friday evening there had been no train arriving or leaving Clerehaven station at the relevant time.

'Did you get a fix on the time from the neighbours?'

'Nothing definite. There's still only the poodle woman saw her coming out of her drive. Late afternoon was the closest she could get.'

'So it could have been five – just before – time for her to get to Chatfield Central for five thirty.'

Annette breathed, 'Five thirty. Chatfield Central. Oh, God . . .'

'Yes . . .'

The comings and goings, meetings and partings: the surge of people on foot, getting taxis, picking up cars, making for the bus station, in such a great tide of humanity, how could an individual imprint their presence . . .?

And the seed, planted in Hunter's mind – if she was meeting someone who did not wish to be seen with her, it was the ideal time and place. If this was premeditated. And something in his bones told him it was.

The evening's briefing confirmed Hunter's gloomy perception that over three days little progress had been made beyond the identification of the victim. In spite of appeals no one had come forward with any information, there had been no sighting of her car.

Never one to discourage his team, he resorted to the cheerful platitude, 'Early days yet, lads and lasses,' and was rewarded with a noticeable refocusing of attention. 'You're right,' he said decisively, as if an unassailable and popular decision had been reached. A few bewildered faces registered alarm (*What have we missed?*); old hands, inured to his non sequiturs, maintained inscrutable expressions.

'You're right in this: we don't know enough about Jaynie Turner and until we do – short of someone walking in here and confessing – we won't get anywhere near who had reason to murder her. So tomorrow, we concentrate on B.N. We've been through her papers till we know them by heart – no trace of a B.N. there. Yes?' On the face of young DC Paul Evans, new to Hunter's team, a troubled awareness moved.

DC Evans, painstaking and literal, with the deeply furrowed brow of the conscientious, said, 'Her papers, guv.'

'Her papers. Yes?'

'Well, apart from the usual things, birth certificate, marriage lines, household stuff, the rest – the family history and local history –' DC Evans' tone grew increasingly bemused, 'well, they just seem to be – well, all about her. Photos, and notes about how people admired what she was wearing and things written on the back of invitations about how everyone had found her charming and –'

'That's because the woman was in love with herself,' WPC Mary Clegg said briskly. In her, cynicism and rock-bottom common sense were combined; it was well known she never allowed tact to get in her way when plain speaking was required.

'Herself,' DC Evans repeated slowly.

'Who else?'

DC Evans frowned ever more deeply.

'Well, think about it,' Mary said. 'If there'd been some frantic feller he'd have shown up by now.'

'Not if he had something to hide.'

'You've got it there, lad,' Mary said kindly.

Hunter listened with patience; his instinct to pair them to work together had obviously paid off. 'What we do know without doubt is that she was very fashion-conscious, always wore gloves to match her outfit, certainly when she was driving.'

'Could her murderer have known that?' DS Hopper asked.

'Whether he did or not, he took advantage of it.'

'That's why her hands didn't show any signs. Then he removed her gloves, took them away –'

'He did. And the bastard who could think to do that wouldn't dispose of them anywhere near the scene where we might find them. He took her handbag, too, remember.'

'To delay identification.'

'And give him a head start. He could be anywhere now.'

It was Annette's turn to speak up. 'She's been in Clerehaven getting on for two years and she had masses of social contacts – but she doesn't seem to have formed any relationships, not anything significant. I mean, we haven't had any best friends – *any* friends really – coming forward to say they knew her better than anyone. At least not so far as we've been able to find out, I know you said it's early days, guv, but surely someone would have spoken up by now. And Mary's right – there's no sign of any distraught boyfriend. A beautiful, well-heeled, unattached woman – and no man around.'

'There could be a reason for that,' PC Bale intervened. 'According to a very chatty lady, did this local history course with her, Mrs Turner was very bitter about her divorce, about men in general, come to that. Never wanted anything to do with them ever again.'

'I've heard that before,' Mary Clegg muttered.

'Yes, a situation that could change, that's not to say it did, but . . .' Hunter recounted his interview with Inez. When he had finished, DS James Collier said:

'She sounds a bit giddy – I mean, she had a conversation with another woman and can't even remember if she said she'd got a date or not.'

'More exasperated than giddy, I'd say. And completely honest. She didn't listen to Jaynie Turner because Jaynie Turner seldom said anything that wasn't trivial or narcissistic, often spiteful.'

'She didn't like her,' Mary Clegg said.

'So you'd scarcely get an objective opinion,' Collier said.

'Do you ever?' Hunter murmured, unheard as voices surged around him.

'Maybe she was being deliberately cagey because the guy's married –'

'That'd be why he won't come forward –'

'– attractive, all right, yes. But I got the impression there was nothing to her apart from boobs and glitter. Who'd want a relationship with a Barbie doll?'

'*Me, please* . . .' A yearning undertone.

'And talking about impressions, no one likes to speak out when there's been a murder, but, honestly, I couldn't find anyone who really liked her.'

This provoked thought and general agreement which someone summed up: 'But it wasn't an active dislike, was it? Not hatred. She didn't have *enemies*.'

'She had one,' Annette said quietly.

'Right,' Hunter called them to order. 'So, here's what we do. Lacking a significant other in Clerehaven, and with her address book gone missing, we'll concentrate our enquiries here in Chatfield for the present. She's lived here since she was a girl, her ex-husband and children are here, this is where, if anywhere, there'll be long-standing friends she confided in. Let's find out who they are and what they know. And, for lack of anything else to go on, we'd better see if we can turn up anything on the mysterious B.N.'

There was something to go on the following morning; slight enough but at last a response to appeals for information, in the person of Fred Armitage, who walked into Chatfield police station.

What he had to report was fed straight through to the incident room where it was logged on to HOLMES and reported with some excitement direct to Hunter by Sergeant Hopper.

Fred Armitage lived in a housing development northeast of Chatfield. He had been born and brought up in Hasley Bridge where his old mother still lived in Sebastopol Terrace – two streets on from Old Park House.

'He visits her regularly when he's home – he's a long-distance lorry driver, that's why he hasn't come forward before. Last time he went to see her was 29th October –'

'The day Jaynie Turner went missing.'

'Right. He always walked, had to pass the drive that goes down the side of Old Park House. Street lights don't reach all the way down, as you know, but he just glanced, in passing, saw a car, pale colour, could have been blue. No, he didn't notice the number, but then it's doubtful he could have made it out from the road.'

Forensic evidence confirmed, as near as possible, that that was when her body would have been placed in Old Park House. Further confirmation followed swiftly from the regular Blakey Estate patrol. Tucked out of sight in the derelict industrial area: the burnt-out shell of a BMW. Nobody on the estate was inclined to volunteer anything in the way of information, but persistent enquiries eventually established that it had appeared on the day following the night Fred Armitage had seen a car parked on the Old Park House drive. It yielded nothing in the way of evidence, not even a scrap of its original colour, but the chassis number was recoverable; a check on the Police National Computer proved the car to be registered in the name of Jane Alice Turner of 14 The Avenue, Clerehaven, Cheshire.

On-going enquiries, centred on what had been, until comparatively recently, Jaynie Turner's home ground, turned up three candidates for B.N. – all inappropriate. A mad nonagenarian aunt, a cousin in Detroit, another cousin retired from the grocery business and wheelchair-bound.

'That's it,' Hunter said. 'What about anything else? Boyfriends, enemies? *Anyone?*'

No one – until Annette produced Jaynie Turner's diary from the Property room and approached Hunter with such diffidence he was prompted to ask, 'What's the matter with you? You look as if you've swallowed a budgie. Come on, spit it out, it can't be that bad. Can it?'

'It's just that – I've been going through Jaynie's diary . . .'

'Ah . . .' Hunter said cautiously, wondering what it could possibly have to tell them. Social engagements aside, all it had so far revealed was a woman so obsessed with her appearance she had little else to do beyond assiduously recording the attention she lavished on it. Combing through it for any possible lead, Hunter's team had moved from amazement – *What's exfoliation?* – to resignation: facials, pedicures, manicures, depilation, aromatherapy, massage . . . It was now widely held that anyone reading through it once more would go insane; some wit had christened it the maintenance manual.

'Well, I could be wrong about this but – B.N. Maybe it isn't N.'

'What?'

'Look, let me show you. At first glance, or even

second, that's what it looks like. But here – look, this entry . . .'

Hunter read it. 'Ninhams – bathroom blinds.'

'It's one of these very posh shops, bespoke bathrooms, kitchens. I couldn't help noticing it when I passed it yesterday and I thought I remembered something like it in here because the name's so unusual, only it isn't Ninhams – it's Winhams. You see, it's the way she sometimes forms capitals . . .'

Hunter looked. In carelessness, or haste, the first oblique slant of the W ran into the next, resulting in a thickening of the first downstroke of N. And that was not the only example. Painstakingly, Annette had searched out more.

'So, you see, guv, it's more likely we should be looking for B.W.'

'Well done, Annette. I couldn't have been told more tactfully that I've made something of a ballocks.'

'Oh, I didn't mean – we all –'

'Shut up, there's a good girl.' Hunter sighed. 'So, back to the drawing board.'

Collier said to Annette, 'How did he take it? Did he fall on you?'

'Oh, God, if only.' Annette spoke from the depths of her professed wildly despairing love for Hunter. 'No, he saw it, of course. Agreed. Said *well done*.'

'He didn't have you over the desk in gratitude for pointing out his mistake?'

'James, if you were straight you'd be bloody vulgar. It was *our* mistake, all of us. If it was. And we can't be sure.'

'Yeah. And we've still got to catch the bastard.'

Chapter Twelve

The patient retreading of covered ground brought nothing to light. Hunter decided it was time to spread the net wider: sub-teams of the murder enquiry team were set up, one – in Clerehaven – specifically tasked to work with the local force. By dint of studying her diary (her address book was still missing), talking to neighbours, making contact with friends and acquaintances, tracing her leisure and social activities, they put together a welter of background information. Unfortunately, nobody had anything to say about Jaynie that everyone else did not say.

Another team followed up with personal calls, amongst them DC Evans and WPC Clegg who found themselves, in the course of their enquiries, at Evelina Barber's Victorian house in High Town. In the exquisite drawing-room with its bay-windowed view of Clerehaven toppling charmingly down to the river, they sat overawed, terrified an abrupt movement would result in the breakage of something valuable.

There were tiny china plates of savouries scattered on occasional tables; on a sideboard a silver tray set with glinting crystal – decanter, glasses. Evelina was expecting visitors but far too polite to make them feel they were creating a log-jam in her social watercourse. 'Would you care for a sherry? No? How silly of me, you're on duty, aren't you? Coffee? No? I can't really think there's anything I can help with, but do ask.'

'You knew Mrs Jaynie Turner.'

'I did, yes. Poor woman, poor woman. We're all so saddened by what has happened.'

They asked general questions, conscientiously took down names that occurred so frequently it began to seem that everyone in Clerehaven interchanged socially with everyone else. When WPC Clegg asked, 'Did she ever mention to you anyone with the initials B.W.?', Evelina thought, a little nonplussed by the unlikeliness of the question, and shook her head. 'No, not that I can recall.'

'That's not to say that she'd say, "I'm going to see B.W. tonight." She'd use the Christian name and – or – the surname,' DC Evans intoned slowly; he had already decided that Miss Barber lived in an atmosphere so rarefied the normal, everyday exchanges might need to be explained to her. 'But you might have to think about it for a minute because you might not recognise the initials, as such, but you would . . .'

Oh, God. Mary Clegg knew it was impossible to stop him. It was like having a wardrobe fall very slowly on top of you.

'Yes, I quite understand, officer,' Evelina said gently, smiling her beautiful smile. 'But I'm afraid the answer is still no.'

'No,' Evans repeated, making doubly sure. 'Mrs Turner never mentioned that you can recall. But what about you, Miss Barber, do you yourself know anyone of those initials?'

Evelina thought again. 'Well, I did, but it was a long while ago, and I couldn't claim to have *known* him, he was not the kind of person who mixed, you know. At least, scarcely at all at first, and then not at all. It was just that he was there.'

Mary Clegg sat forward. 'Where, Miss Barber?'

'At the Lynchets'. But it really was quite a while ago. And I doubt very much Mrs Turner would have known him, she's only lived here – how long? Two years? Less?'

Every movement deliberate, Evans produced his note-book. 'Who might the Lynchets be?'

'Just – people one knows. There's only Nella left now. There used to be her brother, Alfred, and the old lady, their grandmother.'

'And this B.W. Will you give us his name, please, Miss Barber.'

'Benjamin Wright.'

'And he was a member of the family?'

'No, he and Alfred went to school together, I under-stand. He was their guest for a short while, not a relative.'

'Would his home be in Clerehaven?'

'He didn't have a home in England, as I understand. He'd been living abroad for years, Rhodesia, and then it became Zimbabwe, and things were not as suitable, or something. So he came back here and, I suppose while he was deciding what to do, moved in with his old school friend.'

'Where can we find these Lynchets?'

'As I said, there's only Nella now. Their house is further on from here. You see . . .' A graceful gesture to the window. 'If you turn left at the end of The Crescent, then take the first right after that, you'll come to their house. It's called Ferns.' They rose with purpose. 'But I'm afraid you won't have any luck if you're thinking of going now, Nella's in London all day. She won't be back till tomorrow.'

As she showed them out, Mary Clegg said, 'Lynchet. Isn't he the man who writes that soap on telly – about the Toddies? The shops here are full of stuff about them, aren't they? You can't help but notice. Not that I watch but my nieces are mad about them.'

'Wrote. Didn't I mention that Alfred died some years ago? Yes, he was the originator . . .' Nothing in Evelina's voice indicated what she thought of the Toddies but the most delicate expression – something between distaste and resignation – passed across her refined features and was gone. 'They do, however, seem to be self-perpetuating. Nella has taken over the – er – enterprise. That's where she'll be today, seeing Alfred's agent, or the TV company or someone. She is always so occupied, and it's quite been the making of her, looking after Alfred's affairs.'

On the Monday the inquest on Jane Alice Turner was held in Chatfield. When the Coroner had taken evidence of identification and was satisfied all necessary forensic samples had been collected, he adjourned the inquest pending criminal proceedings and released her body for burial.

At the evening's briefing Evans' and Clegg's report of their interview with Miss Evelina Barber caused an upsurge of interest at once quelled by DC Evans' ponderous, 'But Miss Barber is pretty sure Jaynie Turner couldn't have known this Benjamin Wright. He'd left before she went to live in Clerehaven.'

'Collapse of stout party,' Hunter said.

Evans turned the pages of his notebook. 'I don't recall anything about anyone collapsing –'

'Never mind, lad. But Miss Barber knew him.'

'Not as such,' Evans said.

Hunter's eyes narrowed. Mary Clegg intervened swiftly, 'She said she couldn't say that she knew him.' In a devastatingly faithful mimicry she went on, in Evelina Barber's perfect diction, 'He didn't mix. He was just *there.*'

'Where's there?' Hunter asked, diverted by Mary Clegg's unsuspected talent.

She explained about the Lynchets. 'But there was no point in going round, there won't be anyone in until tomorrow. Do you want us to follow up, guv?'

'Don't waste your time till you can be sure of seeing

this Miss Lynchet; and it does sound problematic – still, we'll have to check. But you stick with the house-to-house tomorrow, now you've started the ball rolling we'll probably find ourselves knee deep in B.W.s.' He turned to Annette and Collier, who had also been in Clerehaven, but drawn a blank as far as B.W. was concerned. 'You saw Mrs Bryant?' They said yes, while he glanced at his notes. 'And she didn't come up with this Wright feller? She and Miss Barber and God knows who else are all part of Clerehaven café society, aren't they? She's been there long enough to have known him. And I know she's friends with Nella Lynchet, she was talking about her when I was there on Saturday . . .' He looked up, sensed hesitation. 'What?'

Annette said, 'She says she couldn't say off-hand . . .'

'But she'll try and think. If she remembers she'll let us know,' Collier finished.

Hunter studied them in turn. 'And?'

They exchanged glances. 'She's not telling the truth,' Collier said.

'Annette?'

'I agree. The impression I had of her, when I met her first – and again today – is that she's a very open person. But when we asked about B.W. – her manner changed.' She looked at Collier for help.

'It's hard to say how, it was quite subtle, but definite. Guarded. And I agree with Annette, she'd come across to me before as very direct.'

Hunter thought about Inez, her candid gaze, her readiness to talk. Either she was a consummate actress and had taken him in completely, or she had reason, suddenly, to be less than forthcoming. If these two, with their empathy and quick intelligence, had sensed something – there had to be something there. Interesting. 'I agree, I'd have said she was completely straight.'

'So, we could have imagined –' Annette began.

'We didn't. But it could be unrelated – or trivial,' Collier said.

'What we thought, guv, if you had a word with her. After all, when we spoke to her we didn't have this Benjamin Wright's name.' Annette looked at him hopefully.

'Very well. I'll pencil her in,' Hunter said impressively. The way things were going he had bugger all else to do.

It was later the next morning he found himself at Cremorne. This time he drove, parking at the opening of the carved gates, beneath the sign that said 'Private'.

He was just locking his car when Inez drove out in her Citroën AXGT, braking to a stop, letting her window down. 'Looking for me? I'm sorry, I've got a class in half an hour. I'm cutting it a bit fine as it is.'

'OK. It'll wait.'

'Well, I'll be teaching the rest of today. Then I'm straight off to Lincoln, couple of days with friends. Is it important?'

Conversation through a car window left subtle responses undetectable. 'Not terribly, another time will do.' He stepped back, registering – or imagining? – a flicker of relief. Could she have some reason to mislead Annette and Collier – and believe she had successfully done so? 'It's just – you said the other day, you're friendly with Miss Lynchet, aren't you?'

The slightest hesitation? 'Yes.'

'Benjamin Wright, too?'

The purr of an extravagantly powerful engine drowned his voice. A gleaming green Morgan came zipping through Cremorne; as Hunter flattened himself out of the way, the driver gestured an apology, waved to Inez, performed an expert turn into the road and disappeared.

He cursed himself for his clumsiness; the diversion

had provided enough time for Inez to adjust her reaction – whatever it had been – and for him to miss it.

'Who? Oh, Benjamin . . . gosh, much as anyone
did.'

He was expert at conveying the most scrupulous
degree of charm and reassurance. 'That's all then. I'll see
you when you get back. Cheerio.' But watching, as she
put her car in gear and moved off. Yes, Annette and
Collier had been right. There was something.

Chapter Thirteen

It was a dripping day, everywhere in Clerehaven had the sheen of old pewter; but when he left his car on the unmade road outside Ferns, and walked down the drive amongst crowding conifers and high, secretive shrubs, he had the sense of something brooding in darkness. The house was almost a relief in all its grandiose dottiness, making him smile, before amusement yielded to momentarily uneasy thoughts of mad wives in attics, bodies in cellars . . .

Miss Nella Lynchet, short, beautifully dressed, overweight, plain as a pug dog, was plainly taken by surprise, and gave the overwhelming impression of being far too busy to see him. They stood in a spectral hall of worn, shadowy elegance. From the depths of the house a vacuum cleaner hummed. Hunter had no intention of leaving. Her resistance, like her disagreeably high manner, might have been habitual; if it was specific he intended to find out why.

'Really not convenient . . . So occupied . . . Scarcely knew her . . .'

He registered the surprise of a man totally misinformed. 'Really? I understood that you and Mrs Turner had been friends since childhood –'

'Most certainly not. I don't know what gave you that impression.'

'No, I can't think how it has happened,' he spoke solicitously, conferring on her an importance she clearly felt was her due. 'We had better clear this up, hadn't we?

It wouldn't do to have the record incorrect in a matter like this. Shall we . . .' He looked hopefully around the hall.

'Oh, very well . . .' She marched ahead of him into a room furnished with severe good taste and not much comfort, sat in a heavily carved, straight-backed chair, placed with its back to the wide bay window. She gestured him to a matching chair facing her. He had a view beyond her of weeping, dense foliage, a depressed winter garden with no exuberance of berries or coloured leaves; the greyness of the day clamped over the glass. He could read nothing of her expression; a light would have helped, there were several statuesque lamps arranged throughout the room, but she made no effort to switch one on. In the short transition between hall and drawing-room she had shifted from incomprehension to attack. 'I must register my protest, Chief Inspector, er . . .'

'Hunter.'

' . . . at being subjected to the indignity of being spoken about by all and sundry.'

'All and –'

'Discussed. My name bruited abroad. Vulgar opinion canvassed as to whom I do or do not know.'

He was on autopilot, taking out his notebook, gravely consulting it. They said of him that he trusted his memory, his intuition, but he was a swine for writing everything down. He didn't believe it possible that any living soul could utter the words 'bruited abroad', wondered if he *dared* write them down.

'Mrs Hope,' he said, looking into her set, pudgy face. 'Mrs Bryant. Miss Barber.'

Her glance turned, reassessing; these were her friends, her social equals. 'I can't believe they would gossip.'

'Gossip. Miss Lynchet, may I remind you this is a murder enquiry which we, the police, are charged with the duty of investigating. I must also remind you that it is an offence to knowingly withhold any information that may assist –'

Taken down, but not prepared to give ground, she waved a pudgy hand. 'Yes, yes. I know it's every citizen's duty to . . . and I'm sure that my friends intended not to in any way . . . I am prepared to overlook your . . .' She went on, unstoppably: she was under pressure, being so busy (too busy, it seemed, to complete a sentence) with her late brother's concerns. 'His name . . . a household word . . . and only myself to handle his career . . . All day yesterday in London . . . an onerous responsibility, Inspector, er . . .'

She had forgotten his name – again – and demoted him, to put him in his place; if he sat there much longer he'd be a DC. An impossible woman: high-handed, self-obsessed, finding consequence in the importance of her brother's meretricious fame. For how long? Till the ratings dropped, a new fad displaced the appalling Toddies, then what would she have?

She paused to draw breath. He said, 'So what you are telling me is that you were not friendly with Mrs Turner.'

'Certainly not.'

He waited.

'I knew her. Clerehaven's a small place, everyone – mixes. To a certain extent. So in that respect, communally, I did come across her from time to time . . .' She shifted, uneasy beneath his gaze, glanced at her watch. 'And now, I must really –'

'Is there anything you can tell me about any enemies she might have had? Did she mention –'

'I knew nothing about her private life,' she snapped. He might as well have made an improper suggestion. Perhaps he had.

'In that case . . .' He stood up.

She was on her feet at once, ushering him out, with what perhaps, for her, passed for graciousness, murmuring something about his waste of time, but then, he must be accustomed . . . in the line of duty . . .

The house had been built in the days when ladies in crinolines surged through the front door, side by side by the width of it. Now it opened to nothing more impressive than Nella Lynchet's dumpy figure – and the flood of vaporous light on her face. Nothing could be read on it but the satisfaction that no doubt always followed a recital of her brother's achievements – and the passing relief of ridding herself of an unwelcome visitor.

Pausing between one stride and the next, he said thoughtfully, 'Ah, yes . . . I understand a Mr Benjamin Wright is known to you.'

She had been making to close the door. 'Goodness, Benjamin?' She was distracted, urgent matters awaited her, she could not be expected to give her attention to something so trivial. 'I haven't thought of him for, oh, I don't know how long. He can't possibly have anything to do with your enquiries. He went away – ages ago.'

'Went away?' Hunter said pleasantly.

'Yes, he was our guest, only for a short while. An old school friend of my brother's.'

'Do you have an address?'

She shook her head, smiling with dismissive forbearance. 'Address? Benjamin was someone who appeared and disappeared. Eccentric. Very much a nomad. No, he could be anywhere. Now, if you'll excuse –'

'Would Mrs Turner have known him?'

'Most unlikely.'

'Why is that?'

'She's a newcomer.' If the abrasiveness had not returned, it was hovering. One thing was plain – Jaynie Turner was someone she would rather not know. Because she had involved herself in something as unseemly as murder? Or just personal dislike?

'You mean . . .?' He smiled, politely persistent.

'He'd gone long before she moved here.'

'Ah, I see. How long?'

'What? Oh, seven, eight years. I can't remember.'

'Thank you. Good morning, Miss Lynchet.' The blandness of his manner concealed his brief frustration: what the hell were they wasting their time on, pursuing a man who had disappeared from the scene long before the murder?

And nothing could be discerned in the blandness of her face as she wished him a sharp good morning. She turned away. The light flashed on the pebble lenses of her spectacles revealing, for an instant, the gimlet gaze of her eyes.

Not once had she expressed even a token regret about Jaynie Turner's death.

Chapter Fourteen

Monday found Hunter knee deep in administrative matters; he was a hands-on copper, reacting to paperwork like a tethered animal, and as the years passed the paperwork increased in swarms. A series of meetings kept him at divisional headquarters, increasing the pressure to get on with the job – *how can I when I can't get out of the building for sodding accountants?* At last he was back on the road, ready to pick up where he had left off.

Darkness had already fallen by the time he reached Cremorne. His course through the gardens was tracked by security lights flicking on and off at each separate house; beaming on an antique door, a driveway, a segment of border. Beyond their glare, the massive trunks of old trees stood like guardian ghosts, lamplight shone from friendly windows. He had never been a man for trampling, but here, surrounded by the eerie beauty of a place designed for tiptoeing, whispering, he was excruciatingly aware of his presence and walked softly on grass verges.

At Inez's house the hall light was on; he knocked and waited, knocked again, wincing as sound crashed through the delicate silence, waited, and at last turned away. As he let himself out through the gate of her small front garden, the door of the next house opened and the figure that emerged was instantly recognisable as the absent-minded professor.

'Ah, you're the policeman, I saw you here last – er –

or was it on TV appealing for – er – yes. I say, is Inez all right?'

'Perfectly. I just needed to have a chat with her, but it seems she's –'

'Is it Monday?'

Hunter responded to this apparent non sequitur patiently; a master of them himself, he knew the chances were they could lead somewhere, eventually. 'Yes.'

'The One-eyed Rat. Come this way.'

'The one-eyed rat,' Hunter repeated carefully, resigned to being introduced to a visually challenged rodent. Perhaps his inward sigh communicated itself. The professor gazed him for a puzzled moment before murmuring, 'It's a pub, you see. I shall give you directions.' They were extensive, baffling, the professor led him by the arm to the gates and stood gesticulating, explaining, eventually pointing him bodily in the right direction.

If it was the right direction. Somewhere in Hunter's mind there stirred long-buried fairy tales from childhood where the traveller, no matter that he can see the enchanted castle in the distance, always finds himself walking away from it.

The minute he crossed the threshold he knew himself at home. Inez was sitting near the fire, reading a newspaper. He said, 'Hallo,' quietly and saw, as she looked up, the surprise and guilt and relief on her face. 'I'll go and get us a drink.'

'Oh, no thanks.' She indicated an almost full bottle of wine on the table. 'Do have some of this.'

'I think I'll try the local brew. What's it like, do you know?'

She looked shocked. 'Good God, I'm not man enough to drink that.'

'Sounds just about right.'

He returned from the bar with a pint that gave off

fumes of ambrosia; he had also bought – without asking for and somewhat to his bewilderment – a crackly bag of something. 'The landlord said I'd be wanting this. I don't . . . Do you?'

'No, but so kind.' She put the bag on the floor beside her. There was a blur of movement. The bag disappeared.

'Um . . .' Hunter, taking a seat, leaned sideways, trying to peer beneath the settle.

'Oh, it's all right,' Inez said. 'Just the armadillo.'

'Armadillo. Yes, of course. Silly of me.'

'How did you know I was here?'

'Your neighbour, Professor Brainstorm.'

'He knew it was *Monday*?' Inez murmured. She poured herself more wine then sat gazing at her glass while he studied her.

After a few moments he said, 'You've got something to tell me.'

She gave a small sigh. 'Your truffle hounds are charming, and very polite, but I had a feeling I hadn't put them off the scent.'

Nobody, as far as he knew, had ever called them truffle hounds; he could imagine Annette's yell of delight when he told them.

'But, after all, it might not matter in the slightest, it's only, I was worried . . .' She looked towards the door. 'My best friend is Dora Hope, sometimes she comes in and we have a drink and a chat. If she does come in, I'll have to change the subject, you understand?'

It was the end of a long day; he couldn't enjoy anything more than the peace and comfort of the One-eyed Rat, the superb brew, her company, some intriguingly unknown creature beneath the settle. There was no hurry, she'd get round to it eventually, whatever it was.

'Dora and I trust one another absolutely, but I have this – secret. I regard it not as my own, but someone else's, you see.'

91

'I will when you tell me,' he said pleasantly.

'It's about Benjamin.'

'The disappearing man.'

'Mmm. I don't know how much anyone's said to you, to be honest there's really very little anyone can say. I can only tell you what I've heard.' As he listened, he checked off what she told him against what he already knew: that Benjamin Wright and Alfred Lynchet had been friends since they attended the local grammar school together; that when they grew up, Alfred never married – but Benjamin did. That was new, no one, as far as he was aware, had mentioned that. For what it was worth.

Inez said, 'They lived here in Clerehaven, they had a baby and then, when it was no more than a few months old, Benjamin just – deserted them. Took off. No one knew where, or why. And he never came back.'

As far as Hunter was concerned, this was all academic. Benjamin Wright had been and gone; for some reason his trajectory was important to Inez, otherwise she would not have concealed it from Annette and Collier, or be trying, clumsily, and with some disquiet, to explain to him now.

'But he did, didn't he? Come back.'

She nodded.

'To the Lynchets.'

'Yes. All this is only what I've heard, Mr Hunter.'

'My name's Sheldon.'

'Is it? How jolly nice. I've never known a Sheldon.' Diverted, she cheered up for a moment. 'I'm Inez.'

'A beautiful name. I've never known an Inez personally, only historically, she was –'

'Lenin's mistress.'

'Yes.' Looking at her in her bright, flowing clothes – the richness of turquoise silk, something rust-coloured, the texture of tweed – he could not think of any other woman who would make such a daring mix of colours and fabrics, but she had the confidence to do it. And her serene face . . . the face of a generous and troubled woman. 'He never bloody deserved her.'

'Well. There you are.'

'Meanwhile, back at the Lynchets'.'

'Yes. Suddenly, he just turned up there. Apparently he'd been settled in Rhodesia, he was a civil engineer, I think. Then things fell to bits so he came back to England. He wasn't here long. Funny little man, nervous and withdrawn. But Alfred was his friend and he did the right thing by him, gave him somewhere to stay, till I suppose he'd pulled himself together. Then he just drifted off, again no one knew where, but that was his way. Honestly, he was so insignificant scarcely anyone knew he was here or noticed when he had gone. But now, you've been asking about him so I assume it must be something to do with Jaynie's death.'

'We won't know that till we can talk to him, although I doubt –'

She interrupted him, intent on following her line of thought. 'I can't see what on earth the connection could be, she never even knew him. What it is, when you find him – if you do – will it all come out? About the past, abandoning his family?'

'As things stand, I can't think of anything more irrelevant. But would it matter? To you?'

'Not to me, no. My friend Sam.'

'The young man . . . the shopping trolley.'

'Yes. He's Benjamin's son.'

'I see. And does he know where his father is?'

'Sheldon,' she said helplessly. 'Sam doesn't even know he *is* his father.'

Hunter didn't need to ask, his face said it for him: *Then how do you know?*

'I told you I inherited my cottage from my cousin, Mary Weller. She lived in Clerehaven all her life, and she'd always been friends with Sam's mother, Letty – she was a gentle, helpless little creature, I did meet her once or twice, in passing, so to speak, I can't say I knew her. She was devastated, being left in the lurch like that, but she pulled herself together for the sake of her baby, and quite soon she met a nice chap who wanted to take care of them both. They moved to Chatfield, set up house and in due course she divorced Benjamin and they were married, very quietly.'

'Happy ending.' But he was alert to nuances. 'Why quietly?'

'Because Sam was of an age then to notice things. And Letty had never told him that the man he called Dad was really his stepfather.'

'That situation isn't altogether uncommon. Sometimes, not always, it's done from the best of motives.'

'This was. Sam adored his dad, he was everything a dad should be – made toys for him, taught him to fish, took him to football matches. It was a dreadful blow when he died, and Sam was only twelve. But the relationship had given him a lot – steadiness, strength. He found a mature consolation in the knowledge that he could never have had a more loving father.'

'And his mother couldn't tell him the truth.'

'She couldn't bear to, it would be like taking all that past happiness away from him. And she felt guilty, his real father had been a rotter, she saw that as all her fault – although it wasn't, the wrong people are marrying each other all the time, aren't they?'

'They certainly are,' Hunter – acrimoniously divorced, estranged from his daughter – said neutrally. 'I doubt any of this is going to surface, there's no reason why it should . . .' As he spoke his mind explored possibilities he judged it best to keep to himself for the present. Inez seemed to have taken it for granted that she was the only person to know of her friend's parentage. But Clerehaven encompassed a small area where memories had a long range; Sam's ignorance of his own vulnerability would be pretty thin protection if someone wanted to make mischief. Why anyone should, it was impossible to say, but Hunter had all too often encountered the torrents of the past swirling up in a murder enquiry. 'You said it's not your secret . . . but surely the Lynchets must know.'

'That Benjamin married, yes, and deserted his family, yes. But I can't see how they could possibly make a connection between him and Sam. Don't forget, Letty left here when Sam was a babe in arms; she changed her name on her remarriage. And the Lynchets would never have concerned themselves with her, they were too, in their own estimation –' she gave a polite cough – 'exclusive.'

'Snobbish.'

'You're catching on.'

He could scarcely fail to, having met Nella.

'Anyway, whatever Grandmother and Alfred might have known, I'm sure they wouldn't have told Nella – and she's the only one left now.'

'You know. Would Benjamin have been aware of that?'

'I don't see how he could possibly have been. He never knew my cousin Mary, or that she knew Letty, that . . . No.' She shook her head. 'It was all so long ago.'

He asked, as if by afterthought, 'Is Sam's mother still in Chatfield?'

'Oh, no, there's no danger of her hearing the initials of her first husband, even by chance.' She tried, unsuccessfully, to repress a smile. 'She married again, not long ago. For a helpless, retiring little thing she didn't do too badly collecting husbands. She lives in Spain now with number three. There's no reason any word of this could get to her. Sam goes to see her quite often but what he tells her is just general gossip – especially if it's about someone she might have known when she lived here. But that's a long while ago; even if he did tell her about Jaynie's murder, it would just be something sensational that had happened here. Ah . . .' She stopped speaking, looked beyond him, smiling.

With the unassuming attractiveness and dignity of her age and class, Dora managed to astonish Hunter. Reaching the table, she inclined towards them, lowering her voice to a dramatic undertone, 'I say, do I belong to that famous French family the *de trops*?'

'Don't be so bloody daft,' Inez said equably.

Dora winked at Hunter, went to the bar, returned with a glass and a crackly packet which she put on the floor beside Inez. It disappeared at once. Dora said, 'Hallo,' to no effect. 'Suit yourself, then.'

Hunter attempted once more to peer beneath the settle. 'Is it – er –'

'I should leave him till he's finished that, if I were you, otherwise he'll have your hand off,' Inez said, smiling. She poured wine into Dora's glass.

Dora said, 'Is he arresting you?'

'Gave myself up.'

'You always do. Are you talking secrets?'

Hunter replied, to save Inez the embarrassment of deceiving her friend, 'Stocking up on local gossip. If I get enough I might have some idea what Jaynie Turner was up to.'

'I shouldn't think you'd have a shortage of volunteers – gossipwise. Everyone knows everyone's business here.'

'Not all of it.'

'No,' she said sombrely.

'Mostly,' Inez said, 'what Jaynie was up to was pursuing her obsession. Getting her own back on the Lynchets for not being related to them.'

Hunter's smile said *Tell* . . . This was, after all, Clerehaven, where convolutions and eccentricities abounded, he was more than content to listen. And earlier he would not have thought his time more pleasantly spent than in a genuine pub in the company of a charming woman. Now there were two charming women, laughter ready behind their words, bantering in their friendly, expressive voices, calling each other Index and Door. He didn't ask why.

And they talked. About everyone, everything, unaware how subtly he directed them. They said nothing careless or malicious, never passed off as fact what could be fiction, and they paid him the unspoken compliment of their singular honesty: they would speak like this between themselves, to him because of his function – but never to anyone else.

The armadillo eventually chose his time to emerge from underneath the settle. He sniffed round Hunter's feet thoroughly, and with dignity, then made himself comfortable on them.

'Chuck him off if it bothers you,' Inez said.

'No, it's rather . . . a bit like a hot water bottle. Does he always do this?'

'Only if you pass some mysterious test – don't ask me what it is.'

The friendly face looked up, then snuggled down again. 'Well,' Hunter said, 'I suppose this makes my evening just about complete.'

Chapter Fifteen

Collier drove through Clerehaven's winding streets while Annette checked her notes. They were following any lead from Jaynie Turner's diary of the previous year – the year she had moved into Clerehaven. Annette said, 'Mrs Hanks, 7 Regatta Terrace.'

'I know. And?'

'Just "See Mrs Hanks." No cross-reference. Doesn't seem very hopeful.'

'What does?' James said gloomily. The likeliest contacts – family, regularly seen acquaintances, nearest neighbours – had all been interviewed. Jaynie, it would appear, lived a blameless life, what could be seen on the surface was what there was of it; no whispers, no scandals . . . and yet, in some corner, or broadly exposed to unknowing gaze, her murderer walked.

And it was their job to track him with nothing more to go on than a network of hints, allusions, tenuous – possibly meaningless – connections. Unless her murder was a random, motiveless act – and no one believed that.

'It could be worse,' Annette said darkly. She didn't need to spell it out, at least they had not been assigned the mind-stunning job of going through the labyrinth of rubbish Jaynie had called her research.

7 Regatta Terrace, narrow and tall, with steep steps straight up from the pavement, had a gentle shabbiness, duplicated by its owner, who glanced at their warrant cards and welcomed them into her warm, comfortable

back room. She hobbled badly, had a bright, friendly expression and a small dog that looked distinctly odd to Annette, whose parents had always had Dalmatians. This one might be of unidentifiable pedigree but it was as friendly as its owner and inspected their feet thoroughly and with great politeness.

'What can I do for you youngsters? Will you have a cup of tea – you look froze, it's biting out there. And you're much too thin, miss, but they all are these days. Don't take no notice of him, it's just his way.'

The armadillo had gone to the toy box next to his bed, selected a battered rubber dumb-bell and given it to Collier.

'I say, that is . . . thanks,' Collier said.

'Just put it down, he'll not bother you more,' Mrs Hanks said comfortably, as the armadillo settled himself on her feet.

Not daring to look at Annette, Collier said, 'He didn't bark when we knocked.'

'Never does, except at people he doesn't like. That tells me, you see, be on my guard, then I don't open the door. It's about that poor lady, I suppose, folk say you've been asking everywhere. But, really, much as I'd like to help, I knew nothing of her.'

'She had a note of your name and address in her diary, a year last September. You understand, we have to follow up even the most . . .' Annette spoke on, gently explaining, knowing well how perfectly innocent people were startled out of their wits to be associated with a violent event.

Mrs Hanks sat with her gaze fixed, listening, frowning in concentration. 'Yes,' she said, after a short silence. 'Got it now, love. But it were nothing.'

And it was nothing. Mrs Turner had appeared on the doorstep one day (Mrs Hanks had no telephone), with a notebook and gold pen, seeking information for some research she was doing. Yes, it probably was autumn – the last one or the one before, it scarcely mattered at Mrs

Hanks' age. 'What she were asking was something to do with her folk years gone back. And I'd worked with a cousin or something of hers at Lett's, the greengrocer . . .' There followed the detailed and irrelevant tale Annette and Collier had become accustomed to: who had lived where, married who, prospered, failed – most of this dating back to before the Second World War, or beyond.

'And then, of course, I knew her grandfather – chopped wood at Belham's yard for a living. That wasn't what she wanted to know by look on her face – but he fed his family, and you can't put that lightly by, not the way things were then. They were only ordinary folk, like all of us. Not that it wasn't terrible what happened to her, such a very . . .' Mrs Hanks paused, searched for words. 'Glamorous person, like you see on telly. But I wouldn't . . .' She came to a halt, thought for some time, looked down at the inoffensive dog. 'He barked, you see, so I wouldn't let her in – but, well, young Sam were here. "All right, Mrs Hanks," he said. "You stay there, I'll see who it is." Then he talked at the door, and brought her in, so I knew it were all right. And then he left, and we talked . . .'

'Sam who?' Annette asked, notebook ready.

'Why, Inez's friend. You know Mrs Bryant, don't you? I thought she said she'd spoken to someone official, but p'raps I was mistaken. Takes him out for his walk. Every day, regular as clockwork. Lovely lady. Well, her and young Sam are friends. And whenever Inez is away, he comes and takes him.' Mrs Hanks sat back, folded her hands contentedly. 'Are you sure you'll not have a cup of tea?'

They asked, of course, as they left, if the name Benjamin Wright meant anything. She looked at them from the unplumbable depths of innocence. 'Who?'

On the step she gave them Inez's address and Sam's. 'I can't get about, you see, through my legs, but they're always busy all over the place, and they know everyone, they can tell you lots of things,' she said generously, wondering, as she closed the door, if she should add that they could neither of them stand the sight of Jaynie Turner, nor could any folk with sense. It wasn't the kind of thing you could say of a person recently come to a tragic end.

Not that it would have made any difference to Annette and Collier, they had at least a new name, linked to Inez. Collier said, 'I thought Hunter was going to see her – to find out what it was she didn't want to tell us? He hasn't said anything, has he?'

'She's been away for a while, he couldn't make contact till yesterday evening, after the briefing. He hasn't said anything yet, not to me, anyway. Probably another dead end. *Now* we can cross Mrs Hanks off our list and what's the betting *this* one's going to turn out to be a waste of time. Honestly, James, what are we doing with all these *names* . . .' She reeled off a list of them, impatiently. 'These are just people who know one another. People *do*.'

'Yes, right. Cool it, we're getting nowhere except madder and madder. But let's just – just – follow this one. How will we know unless we try?' And the truth was, they both dearly wanted something to take to Hunter for the evening briefing, for their own sakes, because they were ambitious, and for his, because they knew him well, and sympathetically enough to sense his frustration at their lack of progress with the investigation. 'Cheer up, Annette. Most people are coming home from work now, we might just catch him.'

They did, he still had his coat on, opening the door of his small Victorian Gothic house and standing warily back in its shadow until they introduced themselves. 'Police. That's a relief, I thought you were Jehovah's Witnesses. Come in.'

*　　*　　*

101

It was after the evening briefing that Hunter telephoned Inez.

'Sheldon.' Her pleasant voice was restrained, obviously with effort, and not without incoherence. 'You *said*, you *promised*, and I told you it was – and you said it probably had nothing – but still, you sent them – to Sam –'

'Calm down, Inez. I didn't send them to interview Sam, I didn't even know until just now that they had. Now listen, I didn't let you down, I didn't break my promise. Are you listening?'

She drew breath audibly and said yes in a subdued way.

'I have to follow up everything, no matter how remote, that might provide a lead. These are two intelligent detectives out on the street. *They're out there detecting.*' He spoke with gentle emphasis. 'It's what they're about. I don't know what they're doing every minute of the day. If they pick up a word, a hint, if they decide it justifies further enquiries, that's what they do. It's their job.'

'Yes,' she agreed, sounding, to his relief, like herself. 'But, honestly, talk about tenuous . . . To be honest, I'd forgotten Jaynie went to see Mrs Hanks last autumn – if I ever knew. Sam probably forgot it himself. Surely it was a waste of time?'

'Absolutely. That's how it goes.' Hunter, intending briskness, sounded glum.

'Oh, dear, sorry. Well, not a complete waste, there's nothing Mrs Hanks likes so much as a chat and offering people tea. I nearly had a heart attack when Sam phoned and said the police had been to see him. He sounded perfectly all right, though –'

'He was, wasn't he?'

'Oh, yes. He thought it was a bit of a lark. Well, you've interviewed everyone else, he was beginning to feel left out.'

Hunter was tired, jaded, he had beaten through the

necessary, grubby, dispiriting pattern of the day; he needed to eat, he needed a drink, and here was unexpected refreshment of the spirit, her good humour, the sweet tone of her voice, her sideways view of the world and its delights. He said, 'Inez, you told me in confidence about Sam's paternity – did you really think I would –'

'No,' she said, in a rush. 'No, sorry. It's just that I felt cornered. Having that knowledge that even he doesn't, and having to tell you. Really, to protect him, if I can . . .'

It surprised him, how much it mattered that he had her trust, her good opinion. He would, officially, have told anyone if it furthered his investigation – but he would never let her know that he had. Whatever Annette and Collier had reported at the briefing would be put on HOLMES – this might not be essential to the detection of the crime, but it could have its place in the overall pattern that led to its resolution. This, too, was something she did not need to know.

Jaynie's funeral was held the following day in Chatfield, at the church where she had been married and her children christened. The congregation was large: friends, relatives, acquaintances. Jaynie would have approved their numbers and overall elegance.

Several Clerehaven residents were there, many from the Friends of Clerehaven, including Inez, Dora, Evelina. But not Nella.

Chapter Sixteen

Hunter had highly selected pubs, held dear through unchanging years. To the confusion of many he insisted on calling them all the Frog and Nightgown, nobody knew why. (Any more than they knew why, when he went purposefully about his official business, he instructed his driver, 'The sewing circle. And drive like hell.')

He could find enjoyment with the rowdiest when the mood took him, but Frog and Nightgowns were off the common ruck, refuges where fruit machines and karaoke were unknown; places with excellent ale and quiet contemplative corners.

The Crown and Mitre ranked as such: a Victorian edifice, dignified as a gentleman's club. There weren't many of them left in the city, you had to know where to find them – and Hunter did. In side streets, off quiet squares, havens of polished wood and red leather where the devoted clientele read their papers, murmured conversations, then processed into the restaurant to dine on substantial English fare: steak and kidney pudding, succulent roasts, apple pie and custard, perfect cheeses.

Annette and Collier sat in the bar with Hunter. Authorities on his lairs, they knew – or thought they knew – how to track him through the city by his favourite pubs. This one reduced them to helpless laughter: *Shouldn't we tell them Khartoum's fallen?* . . . *Somebody died under* The Times *last week, they just keep dusting him* . . .

Often, the whole team would drink together, signing off from a punishing day with sometimes exuberant relief – if nothing much had happened, nothing cataclysmic had happened, either. But this was the kind of evening they sometimes shared: a quiet rounding-off drink, then they would go about their separate concerns; three singles, no one at home waiting for them, although there were occasional affairs.

This evening Annette had managed to convey hurriedly to Collier on the way in from the car park, that Hunter had given her to understand that after their drink his evening was occupied. 'Occupied,' she muttered. 'Do you think he's got a date? Who with?' 'With whom. Accusative after preposition,' Collier hissed back. 'Effing pedant,' Annette said vaguely, distracted by Hunter's private life. She was deeply interested in it, long ago claiming (to Collier) a passionate, hidden love. 'You're just a silly, romantic girl,' Collier said. 'So are you, sometimes.' 'Yes, but I'm not in love with my boss.' She had her doubts about that.

From the bar, the swell of measured conversation, the occasional bark of gentlemanly laughter reached their corner. Collier asked, 'Did you see Mrs Bryant, guv? You remember, what we thought . . . Was she holding out on us?'

As Hunter had said nothing at the evening's briefing they had not asked, assuming he had his reasons. Which might be personal, Annette thought, speculating anew on 'occupied'. Inez Bryant was a wonderfully attractive woman.

'Yes, but it's not likely to take us anywhere.'

Some disappointment, more persistence. They had specifically asked him to see her. When they did that, for whatever reason, they were curiously possessive about his response: he owed them his judgement, they wouldn't let go until he told them.

He had given thought to that. He didn't intend telling them the whole truth, but he was adept at manipulating

enough of it to sound sincere and apologetic at the same
time.

'She did recognise the initials –'

'Ah –' Collier murmured.

'– and came up with the same name as Miss Barber.'

'Benjamin Wright.'

'Yep, long gone and completely irrelevant. It was a
compliment, though,' he said, teasing and diverting
them.

They looked utterly lost. After a while Annette asked
tentatively, 'Um . . . what was?'

'Mrs Bryant. She called you truffle hounds.'

She gave a yell of laughter. Collier, grinning but undi-
verted, said, 'But why didn't she tell us, though? About
recognising Benjamin Wright's initials.'

'Precisely because she had recognised them. If she's
not exactly friendly with, she's been known to and by
the Lynchets for quite a while. She couldn't see any
harm in Benjamin – what there was of him.'

'Yes, I picked up those hints,' Collier said. 'Pretty
retiring sort of man.'

'To the point of invisibility. But still, she felt embarrassed, awkward – it was her duty to tell us, but the
most innocent people become reticent when their duty
conflicts with their social obligations.'

'Don't we know,' Annette murmured. '*I have been here
before . . .*'

'*. . . but when or how I cannot tell . . .*' And as he
completed the line, something clicked in Hunter's
mind.

'What?' Collier said, losing track. 'What?'

Annette said, 'You know, that poem of Rossetti's.
"Sudden Light". About *déjà vu*. Oh, you didn't do Eng.
Lit., did you?' She had to get her own back for the *whom*.
'What was your degree? Picture framing?'

'You know perfectly well . . .' James began, then
faltered, looking at Hunter, who was gazing into some
revelatory distance.

That was it. The scene of crime. Old Park House. Jaynie's body had been removed. The sense that had nudged him, and was gone: this had happened before . . .

He said, 'It was getting on for five years ago. 1985. Autumn. A young prostitute, very young, she'd not been on the game five minutes. Her body was found at Old Park House. She'd been strangled.'

Two faces stared at him in silent accusation: *Why haven't you remembered before?*

'Because,' Hunter said resentfully, 'when it happened, I was away at Bramshill on a three-week management course. Three bloody weeks away from the job. They brought in DI Maclean to cover – you never knew him, he retired not long after.'

Annette leaned forward, impatient. 'And we got him? The guy who strangled her? One of her punters?'

Hunter was shaking his head, brooding. 'I'm trying to remember. The whole thing was over and done with by the time I got back.'

'So it was wrapped up. We got him.' Collier said.

'No.'

'But you just said –'

'No, Annette. I said it was over and done with, not that we got him. Just let me think a minute.'

They waited. Hunter took a reflective pull of his pint. Annette was at bursting point when he finally spoke.

'Cold case.'

Detected suspect dead. Collier sat back, deflated. 'Did he top himself?'

'No, an accident of some sort. What happened, it was a few days before we got on to him. This girl was new around there, bit of a part-timer, there wasn't much sympathy for her so when we asked around the toms for information we weren't exactly flattened in the rush – the usual thing, no one knew anything . . .' He paused.

'No one *wanted* to know anything,' Annette supplied.

'Right. We had to keep up the pressure, they were the only ones who could give us some kind of lead. Eventually someone came up with the make of his car and enough of a reg to trace it. But by the time we got to him, he'd been killed. Hit and run, now I come to think of it.'

They sat with their own thoughts for a while, until Annette said, briskly, 'That's it, then. Five years ago. A part-time working girl. A respectable, divorced woman. Same MO, same location. But that's all, there's nothing to connect them, is there? Who was the guy, anyway? Someone local?'

'If I heard his name, I've forgotten it. Local? No.' He sat looking at nothing for a while, pursuing a hide-and-seek recollection. 'No. That I do remember. But I'm pretty sure I know where he came from. Clerehaven.'

There was a short, intensely thoughtful silence. Annette said, as if waiting for contradiction, 'Coincidence.'

'We can't be sure,' Collier said. 'Isn't it worth following up, guv? We could do it.'

'It's problematical,' Hunter said, for all the good it would do. Collier had taken Annette's participation for granted; she had made no objection. Hunter recognised the muted signs of anticipation. Give them an idea and they were like bolting rhubarb with it.

'We're not exactly thronged with leads,' Annette pointed out, unnecessarily.

'Still, I don't want it to take you away from the job.'

Collier looked reproachful. 'You know better than that, guv.'

Of course he did. 'All right, I'll leave it to you, if you think it's worth a shot. But don't make a meal of it because, quite honestly, I can't see it taking us anywhere.'

'That's because we haven't looked yet.'

'There's the old file,' Hunter mused.

Collier said eagerly, 'I could –'

'I said the *old* file, James. It *isn't* something on that implement so dear to your heart. It's up in the attic somewhere, God knows where. It's paper and folders and elastic bands and paper clips. You don't log on, you blow the dust off. All right?'

A waiter passed briskly, nodded to Hunter, who nodded back. Annette noticed the exchange, her mind switching momentarily to that intriguing 'occupied'.

'It shouldn't take much finding,' Collier said. 'And if it does, we can always ask George Withers, he's everyone's folk memory.'

'That's what community policemen are for,' Annette added.

The waiter paused at the group by the bar, murmured something. Two solid gentlemen detached themselves, made their way towards the dining-room, their measured tread, their gravity testifying to a lifestyle of bespoke tailoring and vintage port. They halted. 'Ah, Sheldon, we are too previous . . .'

'Not at all, we're finished now,' Hunter said with a wickedly bland goodnight to Annette and Collier. He didn't look back, aware that they had collapsed against each other, speechless with suppressed laughter.

Chapter Seventeen

The policy of the Chatfield police to hold files for five years and then destroy them went by the board with the move to the brand new subdivisional headquarters and ran into further confusion when records were weeded awaiting transference to HOLMES. Collier accordingly found himself in a room disproportionately small for the volume of paper crammed into it. Patiently, he tracked the file by its divisional crime number and carried it off to Annette. They worked through it together in absorbed silence interrupted only by an occasional comment. When they had finished they looked at each other.

'Well,' Annette said, challengingly, although it was not clear whether she was challenging Collier, circumstance, or her own earlier judgement. 'Coincidence?'

'Coincidence,' he echoed positively. Then, 'Oh, God, I don't know.'

'Neither do I. Let's go and see Hunter.'

They sat in Hunter's office, the file before them. It was not large; he knew they had tooth-combed their way through it and if they had been able to dismiss even the most niggling doubt, they would not have brought it to him.

The victim's life was tragically brief, tragically familiar. Tracy Lyons, only child of a single woman (father unknown) who had died in a house fire when Tracy was eight, had been in and out of care all her young life, absconding from children's homes, drifting into prostitution from the age of fourteen onwards. She emerged from the dark heart of this social deprivation to something like survival: a few years of abuse, drugs, poverty, sexual savagery. Then she had died, at just turned sixteen.

Her body had been found by children playing at Old Park House the day after her death, 12th August 1985. Like Jaynie Turner, she had been strangled with her own scarf but there were two significant differences between the deaths. One was the incontrovertible evidence that Tracy Lyons had been murdered in Old Park House where she was found; the other was the problematic signs of sexual activity: Tracy Lyons' skirt was pulled up to her waist, either she had worn no underwear or it had been removed, there were semen traces, but no evidence of penetration.

Amongst the women euphemistically known as 'working girls', her youth might have provoked jealousy, her aggressive nature did nothing to enlist sympathy: she was a newcomer and the generally expressed hindsight, 'she was nothing but trouble,' turned out to be adequately demonstrated. Without exception the other prostitutes turned their backs on her fate, but unrelenting questioning produced a few stray leads: type and make and colour of car, possible numbers or letters of the registration plate. Eventually, these details were collated to a sufficient degree to enable the police to trace the owner.

He was Alfred Lynchet of Ferns, River Way, Clerehaven.

Hunter said, 'Well, I'll go to the foot of our stairs.'

'I've heard more than I want to know about the elevated, exclusive Lynchets,' Annette said, 'and here's one of them consorting with a teenage prostitute.'

'It happens.' Collier was philosophical. 'That type can fancy a bit of rough as a change. Mind you, murdering her's a bit out of the general run of things.'

Because she threatened him? Because he was unbalanced? Speculation at that stage was pointless. There could be any number of reasons why an ostensibly respectable man became drawn ever more inexorably by his need, his lust, his inadequacy, to degradation and violence. But this wasn't just a man terrified of losing his reputation amongst his community, Annette pointed out reflectively; there was another dimension. He had originated a television series that, at the time, had started on its landslide success; his name might not be a household word, but it was linked with one rapidly becoming one. The Toddies. Whatever anyone thought about them, everyone had heard of them and would, inevitably, hear of him – had matters taken their course.

Hunter reflected on the supercilious woman, alone in the big house, living on her late brother's success as crumbs from a rich table. Had she had *any idea* how close he had come to being charged with murder? Could that cold manner be a form of resistance to the dread of the past coming back to strip her of all she had now? He could not be sure, but instinct told him there was something complicated going on beneath the surface. The disappearing Benjamin, for one. Was there a connection to be made with the present crime?

He picked up the report from the Clerehaven police. 'So, what about this hit and run accident?'

Collier said, 'It happened at the far end of High Town, I know the place. It's a quiet area, a few old houses with large gardens, high walls or hedges. There's some residential, mostly posh homes for the elderly, a few businesses and shops, then the railway station.'

Hunter said, 'There was only one response to the appeal for witnesses.'

'Yes. It's very quiet there that time of evening, dusk, everyone at home. This woman . . .' Collier consulted the file, 'Victoria Slatter, had had a day out in Clerehaven and was walking to the station to catch the last train back to Chatfield. She didn't come forward until she read about the accident in the paper, and the appeal for witnesses, because she didn't know at the time there'd been an accident. What she had seen was a big blue van with numbers H 7 Y tearing out of the side road where it happened.'

'Did she, now?' Hunter murmured.

'She wasn't even sure of the order of the letters, it was just those three registered with her. Of course, Clerehaven ran a check through the local computer – anyone using a blue van. Nothing. Then a brief house-to-house – anyone using a blue van. Nothing. This all happened before the connection was made with . . .'

Collier's voice ran down. Annette was watching Hunter, who was sitting very still, studying the witness statement and almost audibly pursuing his own thoughts.

Annette craned to read; Hunter obligingly swivelled the paper. *Mrs Victoria Slatter, 14 Kitchener Terrace, Browncoats, Chatfield.*

He said. 'That's Queenie Walley.'

Annette read the name, helplessly, three times. 'Er – it says Victoria. Oh, yes, I see, Queen Vic. But, Slatter?'

Hunter, thinking, said, 'Only for a week.'

They waited, knowing perfectly well they had not misheard, trying to work it out. Eventually, Annette admitted in a small voice, 'Give up.'

'An old tom, even then, she'd seen better days, by God. The older she got, the harder she got. Quarried, was Queenie. Granite, wouldn't give you the shit off a shovel. And here –' he looked down at the paper – 'in a fit of public spirit, she *volunteers* . . .' Words failed him, a circumstance so unusual Annette and Collier maintained an awed silence. At last, unable to help himself, Collier breathed, 'Go on, guv . . .'

'She was in and out of the old nick often enough, drunk and disorderly, behaviour likely to cause a breach of the peace, the usual sort of thing. Before your time – but as far as I know she's never showed up here. The

113

thing is, she got married, about five years ago – to one of her punters. It caused quite a bit of hilarity, most of it crude beyond belief. She was getting on for retiring age. Some men like the motherly type, you know, feel safe, or perhaps it's something to do with early potty training –'

'*Guv* . . .' Annette said.

'Yes. He was a decrepit old guy, *and* loaded. He must have been pretty gaga to go through with it, but not so far gone his family could get control of his affairs. They made a hell of a fuss, but he cleared off and did it and within two weeks he was dead. Heart attack.'

'Was it?' Annette asked.

'Yes, all perfectly above board. And Queenie wouldn't have done herself any favours seeing him off – he hadn't changed his will in her favour. His family were in line – as they always had been – to get the lot. Queenie hadn't thought of that – or perhaps he'd told her he'd see she was taken care of but never had time to get round to it.'

'Did she take legal action?' Collier queried, although there really was no point asking: women like Queenie Walley had not the faintest idea how to go about taking legal action. She would assert, loudly and frequently throughout her life, *I'll have the lor on you*. But she knew, as all women of her kind knew, the law was not for them.

'Did she get *anything*?' Annette asked.

'A grace and favour payment. To shut her up, stop her making a scandal. She threatened to turn up at the funeral and demand her rights. She was more than capable of it, that's why they traded with her. It would have been like a charging rhino loose among the headstones. Doesn't bear thinking about.'

'But, guv, what kind of credibility would we give to a witness like that?'

'Nowt, lad, here in Chatfield at the dangerous edge, where we know Queenie Walley. But Clerehaven. They take people at face value there, it's a conditioned reflex. What reason would they have to doubt her? A respectable widow, a concerned citizen doing her civic duty. And her address, Browncoats, it's not much but it's not the pits. There was no reason for them to take her for anything but an impartial, honest witness. I did hear that she bought her house with the proceeds of her – nuptial settlement. The thing was, she just hadn't been married long enough for it to register that she wasn't still Queenie Walley, everyone went on calling her that.'

'So she didn't misrepresent herself when she volunteered her evidence.'

'Not at all.'

'*Why* would she, though? Volunteer?' Annette murmured.

'Your guess is as good as mine.'

Collier said, 'It wasn't as if it was her own patch, where people knew her, *might* have known she'd seen something, maybe got a score to settle, or wanted to make trouble. But where she was a stranger . . .' He consulted the file. 'No, she didn't know anyone, just on a day out –'

'If you're thinking there's a connection –' Hunter began.

'She certainly wasn't on social terms with the Lynchets,' Annette finished.

'No,' James persisted. 'But we know Alfred picked up this young – Tracy.'

'Do we?' Hunter said

'All right. It's odds on. His car was known round the red light area –'

Hunter said, 'Nobody identified him. The descriptions we did manage to get could have been anyone.'

'Yes,' Collier said reluctantly.

Hunter relented: 'But go on.'

'Could she have known Queenie?'

115

'Everyone knew Queenie. Yes, I'd say they're sure to have been known to one another.'

'Well, could Alfred have known Queenie? Could he have been one of her punters?'

'There's a hell of a difference,' Annette pointed out, 'between a teenager and an old boiling fowl. And don't either of you tell me all cats are grey in the dark.'

Collier said, 'Come off it, Annette, we're not talking aesthetic considerations here. It's necessity, you know, for all these pathetic limp Willies – whoever's available.'

'I suppose so . . .'

Hunter said, 'Look, until we get something else and it at least starts to look like hanging together, we can't run with it. There's no urgency in this. When I've got a minute, I'll go round and see the old boot. All right?'

Chapter Eighteen

Collier and Annette asked around the nick, jogging memories of the team who had worked on the Tracy Lyons murder at Old Park House. All they could discover was that there had been nothing about it to make it remarkable, or to strike a chord (other than location) with Jaynie Turner's murder. In the general opinion, 'There was nothing to remember – and bugger all that could be done. It was too late. By the time we got to the feller he was dead and buried. Well, cremated to be exact. And we don't take ash to court. Bit of a waste of resources.'

'Queenie it is, then,' Annette said.

Collier said, 'Browncoats. Where Queenie used to live. I was there today.'

'Somehow I thought you might be,' Hunter said. '*Used to?*'

'Yes. There's a For Sale sign outside her bungalow. I knocked, and hung about a bit till the next-door neighbour came out – thought I was a prospective buyer, perhaps. It seems Queenie's in a hospice and – if you want to see her, guv, you'd better not leave it too long.'

'Me.'

'Well, from what I hear she'll never tell anyone anything, so I don't stand a chance. But she knows you and –'

'Where do you think that's going to get me? Queenie might be *in extremis* but you don't imagine that's going to make the slightest difference to her attitude, do you?'

'No. But what I was going to say was – and *you* know *her*. You've got her measure. You'll know if she's holding out on you; you won't be distracted by – um . . .'

'Finer feelings? Thanks. You've still not convinced me we can run with this.'

'No. But that's what you'll find out when you see her.'

Confronted by such politely self-contained optimism, Hunter wondered why he had the feeling – not for the first time – that he'd painted himself into a corner.

Hunter had said there was no urgency, and when he finally turned up at the Woodhall Hospice, its enveloping gentleness slowed the pace of everyday concerns. He explained himself to the manageress, assuring her, 'I won't keep her long.' 'Oh, don't bother about time, it doesn't matter here. Stay as long as you want, she doesn't get visitors. When she wants you to go, you'll know about it.'

In a spotless room, colourful with bouquets, he found the buxom, forceful woman he had once known reduced to a framework of wrinkled skin, yellow as ancient parchment, a near-bald head and bloodshot eyes; the scent of the many flowers could not mask the smell of the wreckage of a body approaching its corruption.

And he had been right, she had not changed, she had simply pared down to essentials – 'Whatever you want, Mr high-and-mighty Hunter, you'll get sod all out of me.'

'Is there anything I can do for you, Queenie?' he said patiently, safe in the knowledge that there could be nothing – or, if there were, she would not ask him.

She gave him, venomously, her opinion of his capabilities and how he could dispose of them. He made the occasional, unruffled response, listened attentively. Her old sharpness was a habit that was dying with her, she could no more divest herself of it than do handstands; but it was undermined by wandering moments and sudden, bewildered pauses.

He had better use for his time than sit and exchange insults and said so, cheerfully. 'I want you to tell me about Tracy Lyons.'

She looked away. 'Who? Who'd you say?'

Was her deafness the genuine failing of age and sickness – or was it one more desperate weapon in an armoury becoming ever more depleted? 'Ah, her memory's going,' he said softly to himself.

'There's bugger all wrong with my memory. You ought to have one so good, you'd do your job better.'

'True enough. What about Tracy?'

'Poor little cow,' she said, with pathos, and proceeded to paint a picture of a pitiable social reject who meant no harm and deserved better but never had a chance . . .

'Hang on, Queenie, I'll get my violin out. You're the only one so far who's had a good word for her.'

'All right for you. What'd you know about being deprived? Nowt. Them of us as had it hard –'

'Come off it, you weren't deprived. It's me you're talking to. I knew your mam and dad, remember? Respectable working people. You wanted a good time, anything rather than a steady job.'

'Got it, too,' she said, abandoning her claim of sisterhood with the unfortunate Tracy. 'That young slag'd never made owt of herself, no idea. Fit for nuthin' 'cept getting herself topped. Me, I done all right.'

There was something sly in her complacency, an air of being not only superior to a lost, dead girl but, more importantly, clever enough to put something over on him. He regarded her with a steady look that she was free to interpret as reluctant admiration. Her response was unmistakable; in the old days when she had the reflexes to dissemble he would have had to be quick off the mark, not now, now her preening self-congratulation was evident.

He calculated – the wrong guess could lose him everything. 'You know, don't you? Who he was.'

'I don't know nuthin',' she said, immensely pleased.

'Hey, come on. You talked, amongst yourselves, you working girls, afterwards. I mean, one of your own –'

'Own be buggered. We had nowt to do with a bit of a snotnose like that. Had no respect for her betters, she hadn't . . .' She went on in a vein of maundering reminiscence, congratulating herself on professional encounters always squalid, at times appalling, until he brought her back. His mind retained a hint too fugitive for words: something affronted, something vengeful.

'Doesn't matter what you thought of her, you knew what was what. You could describe him, his car, you had a name – it might not have been his own –'

'Told your lot.'

'You told us bugger all.'

'And that's all there was.'

'Right. What it's difficult to understand,' he went on, conversational, confiding, 'is why a man like that would go for Tracy. I mean, look at his background –'

'His fucking background. What's a big posh house and posh old battleaxe of a grandmother to any feller wanting to get it off?'

Not there yet. On the way. 'How do you know, Queenie?' he said casually.

'What? What?' Her gaze swivelled. 'Read it in paper.'

'Oh, it said that? He had a big posh house and his grandmother was a battleaxe. What paper would that be?'

It wasn't that Queenie always enjoyed a fight, it was that she had no idea how to live otherwise than by hostility and obstruction – and she was still acute enough to know she had slipped up. Perhaps she had done it on purpose, she was perverse enough.

'Come on, Queenie,' he said

She gave him a poisonous look. 'Oh, owe you, do I?'

'No. But maybe you owe yourself something.'

A screech. Amusement? Derision? 'And what might that be, Mr Hunter? Do your job for you?'

'No. Finish yours. They've still got away with it, haven't they?' (the *they* deliberately ambiguous). 'You're the only one who really knows, aren't you?'

She had made trouble wherever she could throughout her life, he had after all given her something – one last chance to strike out. Queenie could not resist.

'Course I do. Course I knew who he were. Told me his name was John and he lived in Nantwich. He were sly, and quick. And posh. You have to watch posh ones, they know how to get the better of you. Not allus. If you know what you're about you can put one over. Looked in his wallet, didn't I? No, I didn't take nothing. You don't take from reg'lars . . .'

(That was it – pride, revenge. Tracy had poached on her territory.)

' . . . they bugger off elsewhere. Best hang on to 'em, they're less trouble, you know where you are with them. Told me he was important – well, they all says that. But I didn't know he was to do with the Toddies, invented them, or summat. I didn't know he was *that* important, not till later, when they got famous. I like them.'

'If he was your regular,' Hunter said sceptically, 'how come he was with Tracy?'

'Because it weren't his usual night, always come Wensdays. This was Toosday. I was at our Vera's in Blackpool. Just his luck he picked up that little cow – or the other way round, more like. I can't see him having the bottle to go for a young one. He had that much trouble managing it – well, that'd give her a laugh, probably try to charge him more for the extra hassle – be just like her. That'll be it, take it from me. He lost his rag,

went for her. He were always edgy trying to get it up;
I had a few nasty moments meself till I knew how to
handle him. But her – she'd just make him feel ridiklus.
And he'd never do with that. Always full of hisself, big-
headed twat. No, he did it, all right, and I knew it were
him. And I wasn't going to let him get away with it.
Justice.'

'Justice,' Hunter repeated, knowing perfectly well that
she was too immersed in herself to hear. She told him
how she got back from her sister's the next day and
heard about Tracy – 'People couldn't talk about nuthin'
else – and I knew. Knew it had to be him. And I didn't
waste no time, I can tell you. I was on train and straight
out to that posh Clerewhatever . . .'

Ironically, literally days ahead of the police, Hunter
reflected.

And she found him; using cunning, greed and tenacity she found her way to Ferns. It was a working day,
Alfred could not at that time be assured of an income
from the television series and was still employed in local
government, so he was at his office. Grandmother
Georgina Lynchet was alone in the house. The thought
of the confrontation of two such implacable women left
Hunter momentarily dazed.

'She knew,' Queenie said. 'Minute she opened door,
looked at me. Oh, yes. And I told her, made no bones
about it. "I were aware he diverted hisself." That's what
she said. Yes. Wouldn't credit it, would you. *Diverted
hisself.* Is that what you call it, Lady Muck? Weren't
surprised, neether. She'd got it all out of him when he
got home night before. Mind, she was sort as could get
owt out of anyone. I've never come across such an old
battleaxe, I can tell you, and I've met all sorts. Looking
down her nose at me. "I suppose you've come for
money, woman?"'

Queenie's story, and the relish with which she told it,
contained the tragic elements of an ancient Greek drama

– and yet it was rooted in the commonplace, the every-day instinct for survival of two unyielding women.

'So she bought you off? There and then?'

'No, old bitch. Said if she give me money I'd throw it around and draw attention to meself. What with your lot snooping around, and all that.'

So they had to horse-trade. Hunter, mentally prepared for the details of the transaction, was jolted off course.

'Then that sister of his – Nell summat – come home from work, unexpected, not well. What the old bag called a "megrim". I found out what that were, after. Course, that sort has to have fucking *megrims* – head-ache's good enough for the rest of us. Old bat saw her off. "Go and lie down, Nell – Nellie, whatever. I'm occupied. I'll come up shortly." Off she went, meek as meek, poor specimen of a thing she was.'

Queenie mimicked the whole scene with reluctant admiration. Some of it might be true; however much or little, there was one vital circumstance: *Nella was there.*

'Did the old girl say who you were?'

Queenie stared at him blankly. What had the social niceties of introductions to do with her?

'Explain you in some way?'

Queenie gave him a pitying look. 'Her sort never explain nuthin'. Gets rid of this Nellie, fast as spit. Then tells me to sit there while she thinks. Gets out some paper and writes summat down. And I'm sitting there like a lemon in this bloody great cold room, with her mad royal highness, scribbling, smiling to herself . . .'

Queenie began to wander, became vicious – but for all her confusion, Hunter had little doubt that at some time she had been in Ferns, in that daunting, shadowy room he had sat in with Nella.

'So?' he prompted, after a pause.

'She says, "We will come to an arrangement. I will give you instructions." Yeh, can you credit it? "Instruc-tions, my arse," I says. "S'pose they collars him." Course, she didn't understand, I had to tell her – her

123

sort has no common sense. She says, grand as a bleeding duchess, "I will see he is not apprehended." "Oh, alter the course of justice, can you?" I says. "Yes," she says . . .' Carried along by her narrative, Queenie halted for a moment, nonplussed. She had, for once, come up against a woman of such implacable certitude, she recalled the moment with something like respect.

'And what was the arrangement?' Hunter asked, beginning to guess.

Queenie glared at him. 'I knew nowt about what she had in mind. I'd never have . . . That sort, they're no different nor us, turn on their own kind . . .'

The story came out in fits and starts, embellished with denials and claims of ignorance, but the truth, eventually – if it was the truth – was that once the two women had measured each other's ruthlessness, nothing would divert them from their purpose.

Hunter walked through the hospice's gardens, thinking deeply. By the time he got into his car he had made up his mind. With luck, Annette and Collier would still be at Clerehaven police station. He reached for his car phone.

Chapter Nineteen

'You haven't got a date this evening, have you?' Annette asked Collier.

'You're obsessed with people having dates.'

'I have my reasons,' Annette said darkly: when they had interviewed Inez's friend Sam she had begun to feel distinctly in the way. 'The boss wants us to meet him about eight thirty at somewhere called the One-eyed Rat. It's a Frog and Nightgown by the sound of it. Apparently Inez and her friend Dora go there Mondays,' Annette explained. 'Plus the armadillo.'

The bewildered Local Information Officer, listening, went off muttering, 'And you think our lot's mad.'

'What are we supposed to be doing there?' Collier asked.

'Talking to them, informal stuff. Hunter wants to get as much as he can on Alfred.'

'Ah . . . does that mean –'

'Shut up, before I forget. He said they're a bit knockabout when you get them together, but they're intelligent and observant and between them know just about everyone. The important thing is to find out, without showing our hand, if anyone had any inkling of the business about Alfred's being a murder suspect.'

'Hunter doesn't think so.'

'Well, there was no reason for it to get about. By the time we picked up his trail he was a goner. There'd have been no point in enquiries. One visit from Chatfield CID would be all it would take to establish that, and if it happened at a quiet time, to one of those big houses up at High Town – who'd know anything about it? The family wouldn't need to explain anything.'

'From what I've heard of them they wouldn't feel it necessary to explain themselves *ever*. If he's going after this, do you think it means he's been to see Queenie?'

'If he has he didn't say. And we're doing this in our own time – so is he. You know he won't commit resources to anything unless he's sure – well, he can't anyway, with Superintendent Garrett breathing down his neck about the cost of major incidents.'

'He's keeping something up his sleeve, isn't he?'

'I hope so, James. Hell and death, suppose it's all about nothing – I mean, we started this, didn't we?'

'Mr Hunter told us about this place. We had to come and see it,' Collier lied charmingly to Dora and Inez.

'It's super,' Annette said. 'I'm going to steal that inn sign.'

'People do,' Dora said. 'They're on about the eighteenth.'

They were sitting in a corner, shielded from the next table by a high-backed settle from beneath which came the tearing sounds of the armadillo on his fourth crackly bag. While they talked generally, Annette satisfied herself it was unlikely they could be overheard, and when Inez asked how the investigation was going their voices became quieter, more confidential.

Collier said impressively efficient things about making progress, then: 'As a matter of fact, you might be able to help us with a bit of background. If you wouldn't mind.'

'Try and stop us,' Dora said.

'It's not been all that easy, building up a picture of Jaynie. Nothing in her life points to what's happened – respectable, affluent, social, but . . . It would help if we could find someone she was close to.'

He paused, registered – without appearing to notice – the infinitesimal withdrawal, the briefly exchanged glance. After an embarrassed hiatus Annette leant forwards, said gently, 'Don't feel guilty, with all the enquiries we've had to make, we're bound to pick up vibrations. You didn't like her.'

'She didn't have friends because she wasn't a nice person. It's so awful to say that now,' Inez murmured.

'Yes, maybe for you. But I can tell you, there's someone a great deal more open about it. Ms Nella. What *is* it about Jaynie and the Lynchets?' Annette, primed by Hunter, firmly brought the conversation around to the right direction.

They explained Jaynie's obsession about a family connection, somewhere in the past, with the Lynchets. Dora said, 'There's nothing in it, and it doesn't matter a damn, anyway. The thing is, when Jaynie moved here she needed something to occupy her. She'd always been in awe of the snob value of the Lynchets and she decided to – attach herself to it. And by that time there was only Nella, and she was a sitting duck.'

Inez said, 'Well, there she was, lonely, plain, how could she help being dazzled? Because it was Jaynie who made all the running. Invitations, shopping together, dropping in at Ferns.'

'Honestly, I think it's the one and only girly friendship Nella's ever had. It was sad, really,' Dora said. 'And it couldn't last.'

'No, it couldn't,' Inez agreed. 'Came the great betrayal, only I wasn't here at the time. It happened during the year I did a teaching exchange in America.'

'Well, that's what you claimed,' Dora said. 'You were gold panning in the Yukon, weren't you?'

'Certainly not. I was dancing in a saloon.'

'Oh, course, you've still got the dress, haven't you?'

Almost diverted, Collier stuck to the point. 'You can't leave it there. We may be coppers but we're only human. What was the great betrayal?'

Dora said, 'Nella fell down the back steps.'

Annette stared. '*Jaynie pushed her?*'

'No,' Inez said. 'I've wanted to often enough, though.'

Dora explained patiently that it was an icy, slippery day and Nella was carrying shopping through the back door because it was nearest the garage. She slipped on the steep steps, broke her wrist and a couple of ribs, knocked herself out. 'Just a little later, luckily, Jaynie turned up. She really did cope wonderfully. Rang for an ambulance, covered Nella with a blanket, stayed by her, followed her to the hospital in her car . . .' For a few moments no one spoke then Dora said unhappily, 'This is unchristian.'

'Tell how it was, Door,' Inez murmured.

'You see, she had Nella's keys, she'd taken them while Nella was unconscious, to get in the house and telephone. And while Nella was in hospital – only a few days – she was in and out of Ferns, looking after things. Then, when Nella came home, she organised us all on a rota for meals and shopping and company. Nella never went out of her way to be grateful, ever – the Lynchets took everything as their due, that was the way she was brought up – but it was obvious it meant a lot to her. Things we all take for granted had never happened in that house – people coming and going, concerning themselves with her, laughter and jokes and gossip. And then . . . her cleaning lady, Mrs Waite, told her she'd several times seen Mrs Turner looking through papers in the study. The thing was, Mrs Waite had never been allowed in there – Alfred couldn't bear the thought of anyone touching his "work"; afterwards Grandmother kept it out of bounds, so did Nella in her turn. I don't know how long it would have taken Nella to realise what was going on – that all the while Jaynie had been helping herself to whatever interested her – prying, ferreting around.'

Annette said, low-voiced, 'That really was betrayal.'

'Exactly. Nella couldn't even bring herself to accuse Jaynie, she just insisted she leave, made up something about other arrangements. I went to see her, I suppose just at the crucial moment, and she told me – not much, she's very reticent, but she couldn't hide how upset she was. She asked me not to speak about it, and I didn't. I never told anyone – except you,' she said to Inez, 'because it was just after that you came back home.'

Collier said, 'I would have thought she'd have jumped at the chance to get her own back – let everyone know what a dirty turn she'd been served.'

Three faces turned to him in complete silence. He had never met such consolidated female disparagement.

'It takes a man, doesn't it? Inez said witheringly. 'Listen, for the first time in her life this pathetic woman had a friend, taking an interest in her life, bringing a bit of fun to it and then, then . . .' Words failed her.

Collier backed into the settle, made himself small, whispered, 'Sorry.'

'Inez is right,' Annette said. 'A man would have gone roaring all over the place making sure everyone knew he'd been made a fool of.'

'And as she'd been treated like one all her life by her ghastly grandmother, it's not the sort of thing she'd want to advertise,' Inez said.

'Besides,' Dora said pacifically, 'it was just not the sort of thing that should be talked about. I suspect Mrs Waite got a bit of mileage out of it, but Nella would have put a stop to that. She'd have made it quite plain she wouldn't become the object of talk.'

A fleeting glance between Annette and Collier carried the message: the Lynchets seemed to have a talent for keeping the lid on their affairs.

'Of course,' Dora went on, 'no one could help noting they'd stopped being friends, but people were pretty tactful . . . And then Jaynie got into her stride with her researches and got on everyone's nerves.'

'This local history thing?' Annette asked.

'Yes. She had a massive folder she'd open and every-one would be fighting to get out of the room. You just didn't know what she'd produce out of it. She said such hurtful things to people, and it began to get embarrass-ing –'

'Digging up people's pasts?' Collier suggested.

'Oh, mostly silly things, nothing anyone bothered about much, a little hurt pride here and there. No, she became more and more spiteful to Nella.'

'Because Nella had given her the bum's rush?' Annette said.

Inez said, 'Yes. If you can't join 'em, rubbish 'em. Mind you, she genuinely did think the Toddies were marvellous – if you can believe that –'

Annette thought of the overdressed dolls, the garden with its mooning gnomes. Yes, she could believe it.

'– she felt she had a claim on Alfred's, what? Kudos.'

'She knew him, of course.' Collier prompted unob-trusively.

'Well, years and years back. Jaynie's parents moved away to Chatfield when she was only a schoolgirl.'

'Childhood sweethearts?' Annette hazarded.

This drew a concerted reaction: '*Alfred*! Ugh . . .'

Annette said, 'Ah, he wasn't a ladies' man.'

Inez said, 'That's just the trouble – he thought he was. Insinuating gallantry. Always trying to get too close –'

'Any excuse – stairs, chairs – arm round the waist –' Dora said.

'Hand beneath elbow. *Damp* hand –' Inez, interrupted by Annette's yell of horrified laughter, said, 'You know the type.'

'Oh God, don't I.'

Collier said, 'Did he have *any* girlfriends?'

'Is this male solidarity?' Dora asked kindly.

'How unlikely can you get,' Annette murmured, heard only by Collier, who trod on her foot.

'If he had, no one knew about them,' Inez said. 'He used to partner Nella occasionally, very condescendingly. She thought it was wonderful, poor thing.'

Dora said, 'He'd never have got anyone past Grandmother, anyway. As far as she was concerned, no one was good enough for him. He agreed, of course.'

'You amaze me,' Annette said. 'I've had completely the wrong impression. I would have –' She stopped, waved to Hunter as he came in.

He went to the bar, gave an order and came over, carrying a crackly bag which he put on the floor beneath the settle, and said, 'Hallo, there,' as it was whisked away. *Ahhh* . . . Annette whispered.

Dora said, 'You'll find him dead under there one of these days. OD'd.'

'Probably his idea of doggy heaven,' Hunter said.

The landlord appeared with a tray: wine for ladies – 'Beer for chaps,' Hunter said to Collier. 'Local brew. What do you think?'

'A worthy Frog and Nightgown.'

Inez and Dora looked too intrigued; to deflect them Annette said to Hunter, 'I'm just learning how completely wrong I've been – about Alfred Lynchet.'

Hunter looked politely interested. A gleam in his eye said, *Good on ya, gal.*

'Well, I had this picture of a feller – mature, yes, but older men can be so sexy – dashing, witty . . .'

She paused, stared at by Inez and Dora. 'The dear girl's not well,' Dora murmured.

Inez leaned forward, whispered, every word perfectly enunciated. 'He was a nerd. Of the very first order.'

A pause. Collier put in, with deliberate inadequacy. 'Not the toast of Clerehaven café society?'

'Assignations, affairs? Delicious hints of scandal?' Annette asked hopefully.

'*Scandal. Alfred* . . .' Jointly, incredulously. Then Dora,

'Grandmother would kill rather than allow the Lynchet name to be brought into disrepute.'

'If he didn't have girlfriends,' Hunter said prosaically, 'did he have boyfriends?'

They considered, briefly. Dora said, 'No . . . That would have registered, over the years, wouldn't it?'

Inez muttered, 'Personally, I think he'd have had anything, given the chance.'

'What I don't understand,' Annette persisted, 'is how a man could create – well, whatever you think of the Toddies, they're enormously popular –'

'That's a guarantee of excellence?' Hunter murmured.

'No, of course not. But he must have had empathy, wit – personality, for heavens' sake. Wouldn't you say? Well, how could a man, who you say was an utter bore, create them?'

'That's what we'd all like to know,' Inez said.

'What are you getting at?' Collier asked innocently.

'Look,' Annette said to Dora and Inez, 'you didn't know he had talent. So there was something in his character that wasn't – evident. He had something –'

Inez said, 'You're taking a rather romantic view of this, I'm afraid, Annette, and it's awfully misplaced. He was . . . repressed, I suppose. Panting and creepy.'

Dora said, 'Maybe he would have made a good husband and father but he never had the opportunity – and, believe me, Grandmother would never have let him escape her influence. And maybe he didn't want to, he could cope with his world as he knew it.'

Annette leaned forward. 'Go on.'

'Well, like a lot of inadequate men he was extremely vain, always hinting he was pursued, sought after, had to be careful not to fall into some unscrupulous woman's hands. But that, poor man, was his fantasy. He never had to prove himself.'

For Hunter, behind this pleasant, gossipy atmosphere,

an echo – Queenie's failing yet harsh voice: *He had that much trouble managing it . . . he were always edgy, trying to get it up, I had a few nasty moments meself . . .*

Inez said drily, 'Wonderful psychological profile, Door. The truth was he was a nerd.'

Chapter Twenty

Annette and Collier saw Hunter early the next morning and gave him a brief run-down of what they had learned before he arrived at the One-eyed Rat. When it came to Nella's accident, they were all of the same mind; as Hunter put it, 'So Jaynie had the run of Ferns – and if there'd been any skeletons in cupboards she could have had them falling out all over the place.'

'She did – well, little scraps of information here and there – that isn't to say there wasn't a lot more in her "research" folder,' Annette said.

'And everything on the Lynchets has gone missing,' Collier added.

Hunter said, 'But we don't know when. Before – after her murder? Did she take it with her when she went out that last time? Did someone get in the house and remove it? Who had entry to the house?'

'The cleaning lady's out,' Annette said.

Hunter brooded for a moment. 'Whatever, we need to ask Ms Nella a few questions. I want you both to go and see her this morning.'

They looked surprised. 'But, guv, we assumed you . . . You've seen her once.'

'Yes, and I know what I think. I want your opinion.'

'Do we ask her about Alfred?'

'Discreetly. We're not showing our hand about that, yet. Hint, see if it unsettles her. Say there could be new evidence about his death. If she wants to know what,

say you're not at liberty to divulge it yet – oh, something . . .'

'It's still being evaluated,' Annette recited.

'Fitted into the larger picture,' Collier continued,
then looked at Hunter more keenly. 'Is there? New
evidence?'

'Oh, yes,' Hunter said blandly, and told them about
Queenie. When he had finished he said, 'Stop jumping
up and down. Just because the old girl's at death's door,
there's no guarantee she's telling the truth.'

'Do *you* think she is?' Annette said urgently.

'Bits of it, for sure, but . . . she could be just making
trouble.'

Collier frowned. 'Why should she?'

'You know better than to ask, James – she doesn't
have to have a reason,' Hunter said flatly. 'Listen. I'm
going to describe Queenie to you as I knew her five
years ago – it's no good you going to see her, she's
unrecognisable from the woman I knew. I asked her
what she was wearing when she went to Ferns –
because she's a cunning old basket and I knew she
wouldn't go there in her tart's outfit. Mind you, her idea
of a respectable appearance isn't necessarily anyone
else's, but she knew enough not to be conspicuous or
have the door shut in her face . . .'

They listened carefully, following his words and, as
closely as possible, his thought. Finally, Annette said,
'Nella came home – while she was there.'

'According to Queenie. That's something I want you
to find out. Does Nella admit seeing her, can she in any
way account for her – then, or later? Tread softly, both of
you. We might, here, be on the way to solving two
murders.'

'Guv, do you think . . . Benjamin –'

'Right, Benjamin. I want you to use him as your
approach *only*. Ms Lynchet's pretty high-handed, she's
going to slap you down because she's already told me
about him – you'll be wasting her precious time etc.

Apologise and back off, that'll give her a false sense of confidence. Then change tack. Start with Alfred, then Queenie. Now, Annette, this is where I want an input from your feminine intuition. You know I respect it.'

He did, it was not the first time – neither patronising nor cynical – he had asked for her response; he knew it to be more subtle than any man's, he understood there were areas of a woman's emotional psyche no amount of analytical expertise could fathom. 'We're dealing with such diverse females here: Nella and Jaynie, the old matriarch, raddled old Queenie. If we do it right, we can fit them together to make a picture.' Then sending them away, with their enthusiasm and expectations, 'Off you go,' he said, adding, 'my lambs,' under his breath. Because they were going to the slaughter and it was Nella who would have their hides.

They were intelligent and tough, but they lacked the depth of experience to read a woman like Nella, and they were too young to have developed the resolute patience that was the gift of years. She would instantly put them down as subordinates; brush aside their enquiries as a mere matter of form and – whether or not she had anything to hide – intimidate and command them. The last thing she would expect, after such a triumph, would be a return visit from him.

Detective Chief Superintendent Garrett had been on leave, enjoying a surfeit of golf that was guaranteed to put him in a decent frame of mind for weeks. Unless something catastrophic happened. Hunter, sincerely hoping he was not that something, received a genial response to his suggestion he 'drop by as he was passing'. Taking the Tracy Lyons file with him, he dropped.

Garrett looked through it, listened to what Hunter had to say about Queenie, thought for a moment and said mildly, 'When I was a lad I had a Staffordshire bull terrier. Once it got its teeth into something you had to knock it unconscious to let go. I wonder why it reminds me of you?'

'It's the Queen Anne legs.'

'So far, Sheldon,' Garrett continued in the same vein, 'you've come up with a man who left the area years before the crime, a dead man and a near defunct old pro who's probably spinning you a line.'

Concession was in the air. Hunter thought back to the rambling, disjointed conversation. Take away the digressions and he was sure he had got at whatever facts were there. 'Some of it has to be true.'

Garrett raised an eyebrow.

'She's been in that house – Ferns. She could only describe it in general terms, so it could be any house of that type – but she hasn't the kind of background to know that. I've never met the old grandmother, but from what I've been told, Queenie had her to the life.'

'Ah, yes, the grandmother. She's dead, too, isn't she?' Garrett remarked, in passing, as he studied the file. 'You believe Alfred was one of Queenie's regulars. He just happened to change his habits the night she was away.'

'That might not have been the first time, he could have done it before.'

'But she felt sure enough of herself to go to Clerehaven in an attempt to blackmail him. Run that past me again.'

'She'd had her hopes dashed with her "marriage". She'd got something out of the relatives but no hope of anything else. She tried. Made a nuisance of herself but they sorted her out. She was pushing middle age, losing whatever pulling power she'd once had. She wanted security, the convenience of a few amenable punters. She was ready to have a go at anything. This just fell into her lap, she saw a chance and grabbed it.'

'Did a deal with the old girl? Doesn't that strike you as a bit odd, Sheldon? A highly respectable ancient lady starts trading with a prostitute the instant she turns up on the doorstep.'

'No. She's not going to shut the door in her face and let her wander off God knows where with her accusations. And the old grandmother knew – she got it out of Alfred the night before. She'd always known he was up to something on a regular basis; men being men as she was probably brought up to believe, it could only be one thing. And she could weigh up the sort of woman she was dealing with.'

'So Grandmother procures a van and careers off in it, running down her own –'

'There probably wasn't a van –'

'There was bloody *something*, Sheldon. He didn't flatten himself into the tarmac.'

'No, of course not. Queenie's instructions from old Mrs Lynchet were these. She was to come to Clerehaven again the following day, do whatever she wished, walk up to the railway station at a specified time. Catch the next train back to Chatfield. As soon as the accident was announced in the paper and an appeal for witnesses, the old lady would phone Queenie. Who would present herself at Clerehaven police station, a respectable, middle-aged widow, who saw on the day in question –'

Garrett read from the file, '*a big blue van with the registration containing H7Y tearing out of the side road where the accident happened.* And Clerehaven go off on a wild goose chase –'

'After a vehicle that never existed. I don't think it occurred to Queenie until later how canny the old grandmother had been. By implicating Queenie she put the frighteners on her about going to the police or attempting any more blackmail later. To cover herself, Queenie swears she didn't know what the old girl had in mind –'

'Did she?'

'If she knew, or guessed, it wouldn't have made any

difference. She pretended to be shocked when she realised, after the event, but she said something to me about "we're all the same, really." I think she saw herself getting revenge on a superior class. I've been doing some digging; someone who knows the family well told me that Grandmother would kill rather than allow the Lynchet name to be sullied.'

'That's not corroboration.'

'No. But it's a viewpoint. And anyway, Grandmother couldn't drive . . .' He paused for a moment, added blandly, 'Nella can, though.'

'Where was she when he was killed?'

'That's something we need to find out.' Hunter waited, allowing Garrett to mull this over for a while before adding. 'So could Benjamin.'

'He, I might remind you, had buggered off beforehand.'

'He was always buggering off.' Hunter did not feel it necessary to enlarge on what Inez had told him. 'They could have known how to contact him – enlist his help –'

'To run down his best friend?' Garrett sounded incredulous.

'Listen, we're dealing with a uniquely weird bunch here. And might it not depend what was on offer? Benjamin was down and out by all accounts, a no-hoper.'

Garrett put his head in his hands momentarily; but Hunter knew his man: he was still listening, they were still trading. Garrett said patiently, 'Has it occurred to you that maybe Alfred Lynchet was killed by a hit and run driver?'

'Conveniently.'

'Mmm . . . If you're after a review of the Tracy Lyons murder, HQ CID should do it.'

'That's not what I'm asking for, not yet. You know certain aspects of evidence could affect the present investigation.'

'Well, yes . . .'

'And if it works, there'll be a bonus: two detected murders for the price of one.'

A momentary gleam in Garrett's eye.

'Look, what I suggest, we'll do some checking, then I'll go back and see Queenie again. Anyone else goes she might change her story completely, I wouldn't put it past her.'

'To put it plainly, Sheldon, you want a bit of rope.'

'That'll do nicely, sir.'

Chapter Twenty-one

In the Wise Owl bookshop, Inez set down two bags of shopping and browsed – a peaceful pastime shattered by the commanding voice of Nella berating some unfortunate assistant.

There sprang at once into Inez's mind: Something She Had Not Done.

It concerned Hatchcliffe Hall, a pocket-sized, exquisite eighteenth-century house. Inez had bemusedly found herself on some committee as co-ordinator of cultural events; as she couldn't remember volunteering, she could only think she must have been drunk at the time. She did her best. The latest venture was an evening's entertainment by a performance poet. In her official capacity, Inez had interviewed him: a gentle, middle-aged man as fine as worn silver, dressed like a medieval alchemist, he played the lute, sang and recited. She was entranced by him.

Nella was presenting the evening and, ever more common now, had left all the donkey work to someone else. She needed details: his career, achievements, where – in her own words – she could interface with him. What she did not hesitate to point out was that her importance equalled his and she must be seen to be doing a professional job. Inez was supposed to supply her with the details; Nella had already mentioned the matter in conversation, left a message on Inez's answerphone. It had slipped Inez's mind; she felt miserably guilty and had no possible excuse.

Assaulted by Nella's irate and commanding tones (surely she was getting *louder?*) she gave in to panic and ran for it, dodged round the nearest book stack, turned towards Railways and Mythology and ran straight into two small children. They went down in a heap: books, bodies, shopping. 'I'm so sorry, kids. Are you all right?'

From underneath somewhere a small, squashed voice said, 'My *arm*. You're *heavy*.'

Their mother hovered, 'Quentin, don't be rude.'

'No, he's not, it's all my fault, I'm an elephant.'

Nella pounced, the tangle of bodies might not have existed, her attention was so entirely on her own concerns. 'Inez, I left a message for you . . . Really, people shouldn't have answering machines if they don't utilise them. I'm in such demand I'd be lost without mine, but I do use it correctly –'

'Yes, no, I'm sorry . . .' Inez, crouching, apologised comprehensively to Nella, mother and children, who were politely helping her collect her shopping. They handed her the box of fudge she had bought to cheer up Mrs Hanks after a nasty cold – 'No, here, you have it, my apology for barging into you – *Yes, all right, Nella* –'

'Look here, Inez, it's all very well for you, but I have to find time in a crowded schedule –'

'Fudge. How kind. Quentin, Jeremy, say thank you. But really, you needn't –'

'Please, I feel so clumsy. They've not made a scrap of fuss. I would, if I fell on me.'

This delighted the boys, who were led away giggling, clutching the fudge, enacting how they could *fall on themselves*.

Nella bore down unrelentingly. 'I haven't *time* to see to these things myself, but I am at least aware of my obligations as Alfred's representative, that's why I take these engagements on. But I shan't be available after Wednesday, I have to go to London to a very important meeting with my agent . . .' She continued to account for herself, at length.

Inez noted ironically that Alfred's agent had now become Nella's. Could it be that her fixation was turning into something more serious? She had certainly been different lately, edgy and arrogant, determined to impress ever more stridently upon anyone who would listen the importance of her status, the unassailability of Alfred's reputation.

At the evening briefing in the incident room at Chatfield subdivisional headquarters, Annette and Collier reported, economically and rather defensively, their interview with Nella. She had been uncooperative and at times downright rude. Very insistent she be given any information regarding her brother's death.

(A puzzled murmur swelled, travelled round the room. Hunter said, 'Hang on, fellers. In a minute.')

But that, Collier observed ruefully, was because she was a bit unhinged when it came to her sacred trust in managing Alfred's fame.

'I know, I've heard her,' Hunter said. 'What did she have to say about Queenie?'

'She claimed not to remember that far back, might have been a cleaning woman Grandmother was interviewing. She wanted to know what we thought we were doing expecting her to concern herself with long ago domestic matters.'

'When we should be out catching criminals,' someone intoned. Annette and Collier nodded, tight-lipped. Their bruises might not be too evident, but they were there, all the same.

DC Paul Evans asked ponderously about Alfred, 'Would this be the Mr Lynchet, brother of Miss Lynchet, who died some time ago – Mr Lynchet did, I mean. I've heard some talk of him as inventing those Toddies, but I don't see the relevance –'

You will, Oscar, you will, mingled with cries of *Put a sock in it, Paul.* 'Oscar who?' Paul asked Mary Clegg; she was the only one with the patience to answer his questions. This time she shoved a stout elbow in his ribs to silence him while someone asked clearly, 'What's going on, guv?'

'Nothing yet, but there is the possibility of a new turn. A link between the Tracy Lyons murder at Old Park House in August 1985 and this one.' Into a concentrated silence he gave a rapid overview of Queenie's involvement. 'This has undoubtedly given us something to explore, but that's just what we're going to do at this stage, because, bear in mind, we've no hard evidence. So, we'll take it steady and get started on some backtracking.'

He assigned new tasks: ascertain if Queenie was at her sister's in Blackpool the night Tracy was murdered; find out if Alfred Lynchet would still be at his job in local government when Queenie claimed to have called at Ferns. He kept to himself for the present the question mark in his mind: where was Nella the evening her brother was killed?

Two men on his present team had worked on the Tracy Lyons murder; he sounded them out. One had nothing to contribute beyond what was in the file. The other, DC Dawes, had called on Grandmother Lynchet when Alfred had finally been traced as a possible suspect. Hunter asked him about his interview with the old matriarch.

'As if it wasn't bad enough getting there and finding the bloke was already a goner . . . She'd have frightened the life out of me anyway, guv . . . I never want to go through anything like that again.' Hunter asked if he thought the old lady could have suspected Alfred's activities with prostitutes. DC Dawes thought heavily for a few moments. He was conscientious and one hundred per cent reliable, but he was never what anyone could call perceptive. 'Honestly, guv, all I remember about that was she reminded me of those cranky old aristocrats in old British films. Hardly gave me a chance to get a word out, and more concerned we were badgering her when she was in mourning. Threatened to write to the Chief Constable. Yes. Friends on the police authority and God knows where else . . .'

It was late when they dispersed. Annette and Collier were waiting, purposefully; they had a score to settle. 'OK. Frog and Nightgown,' Hunter said but he was called away to the phone as they set out.

They were waiting for him, his pint ready. He took a pull, murmured, 'Medusa, wasn't it? Anyone who looked at her turned to stone.'

'Yes, but you didn't warn us to take a mirror,' Annette said accusingly.

'What . . .?' Collier said, looking from one to the other.

'Nothing. Just that two can play at non sequiturs.'

Hunter laughed out loud. 'Come on, you've survived. I didn't want you to be on your guard.'

'It wouldn't have mattered, she'd have probably eaten the sodding thing anyway,' Annette muttered.

'I've lost my place,' Collier said.

'It's a Greek myth. Annette will tell you later,' Hunter said.

'Honestly, guv, when we were talking in the One-eyed Rat, with Inez and Dora – we'd got a picture of someone pathetic, vulnerable –'

'I think she is, that's why she's on the attack.'

'She was that all right, shot us down in flames straight off – "There is no point in coming here to question me about Benjamin Wright. I said all there is to say when one of your men called." *One of your men,*' Annette whispered. 'It took a minute before I realised she meant you, guv.'

Collier said, 'So we did the oops, er, we-seem-to-have-slipped-up routine.'

'Which, of course, would gratify her no end.'

'She was just about to order us off her doorstep, so we did a sort of bumbling making up for lost ground and said we'd like to ask her a few questions about her brother's accident. That got us into the house, at least. Anything to do with him seems to arouse all her protective instincts.'

'Or self-protective,' Hunter murmured.

'What have you got in mind, guv?' Annette asked.

'All she is, what she is, everything she is, depends on him, on his honky-tonk fame.'

'That's why she makes it out to be something so special,' Collier said thoughtfully. 'She'd despise anyone else for creating that load of codswallop –'

'You mean, anything that threatens him, threatens her.'

'She's the only one left, isn't she? If anything surfaced about Alfred now, how would she cope with it?'

'You mean she might know – or suspect – there was something fishy, that's what makes her so defensive.'

'Defensive, is that what you call it?' Annette said. 'She's a Lynchet, I think she'd just ignore anything she couldn't accept. Wave it out of the way and carry on regardless.'

They were thoughtful for a while, then Hunter asked, 'Was she telling the truth about Queenie?'

'It's hard to say. She was obviously put off her stride when we asked, but that could be because she was concentrating on Alfred – and, as you said, as far as he's concerned she's got tunnel vision. I had an odd feeling . . .' She looked at Collier.

'Yes, so did I. But maybe it's the house, it gave me the creeps.'

'Me, too,' Annette said feelingly. 'Do you think there's anything else you can get out of Queenie?'

'Not now,' Hunter said. 'That phone call I had to take . . . It was the hospice, I'd asked them to keep me informed. Queenie, they tell me, passed away peacefully. It's about the only peaceful thing she's ever done.'

'Well, there we are,' Collier said inadequately.

'What now, guv?' Annette asked.

'Garrett doesn't want to commit himself to running with this. He'll give us some leeway, but – it's steady as you go, chaps. And after all,' he smiled at them, 'it was you two got us where we are now.'

Chapter Twenty-two

Shrugged into his British warm against the harsh day, Hunter trudged down the driveway of Ferns contemplating the lonely, mad-looking house at the end of it. In the cavernous porch he rang the doorbell, waited.

She had not expected to see him; after a fleeting, curiously hunted look, her face closed. There was a catch of breathlessness in her voice before it steadied. 'I have to warn you, officer, I shall be contacting my solicitor about this continued harassment.'

'Harassment? Miss Lynchet, I'm afraid I'm at a loss –'

'If you tell me you don't know two of your inferiors called yesterday, my opinion of your incompetence will be even lower.'

'Inferiors,' he repeated slowly, frowning in concentration. 'No, I don't know any of those. I understood two CID –'

'I am not here to bandy words with you.'

'No, indeed, we're both busy people. If I may come in.'

'No, you may not.'

'As you wish. Then I must ask you to accompany me to the police station –'

She gasped. 'What?' Stared, received no enlightenment, said angrily, 'What on earth for?'

'To answer some questions.'

'*Oh* . . .' She flung away, marching ahead of him into the drawing-room.

Sunlight bitter as lemons found its way in through the windows, outlining the dark, bulky furniture, glazing the surface of crowded Victorian paintings. She stood, hands clasped: tense, ready. As a boy on a roaring council estate he had seen women like that, women in worn clothes and aprons, ready for battle. Given an implement to hand – a broom, a shovel – it was odds on that sooner or later they'd hit out. He doubted Nella would so far forget herself, but he measured the distance to the poker, out of habit.

He sat down, uninvited, said, 'Thank you,' politely; took his time patting his pockets for his notebook, drew it out. She made an exasperated sound, sat down in a ponderous armchair positioned sideways to him – a ploy that failed. Her chair was too heavy for her to move; he was better placed in one of the high-backed, carved chairs. He manoeuvred it easily and sat, notebook ready, looking into her face.

She had become very correct. 'I understood from your – subordinates – that you have fresh information about the accident that caused my brother's death.'

'Ah, no, that wasn't what they said. They hoped you would be able to answer some questions because it is just possible a new avenue could be opening up which might throw some light on the event.'

'That,' she said acidly, 'is just the sort of meaningless jargon they came out with.'

'Excuse me. They asked you . . . what?'

'Well . . .' She thought for a moment. 'They asked . . . had anyone strange been seen about at the time – that's certainly for your people to find out. I can't go round knocking on doors, can I?'

'Absolutely not.'

She gave him a sharp look, continued. 'They asked had Alfred seemed upset beforehand. No. Had he received any strange telephone calls? No . . .'

He recognized the smokescreen behind which her

responses were assessed and unasked questions lurked. She was quite right: meaningless jargon.

'It was impossible to make out a word of sense. If that's the way you conduct your enquiries I'm not surprised the detection rate is so abysmal. I suppose it's too much to expect you've come to tell me you have at last found out who was responsible for Alfred's death.'

'No, Miss –'

'Of course not.'

'And can you tell me where you were the evening it occurred?'

'What?' She stared at him, too astonished to say anything else.

'You will, of course, remember . . . To receive such upsetting news . . .'

She looked around the room, seeking reassurance in the familiar. 'I didn't.'

'I beg your pardon?'

'Not that evening. Er . . . when it happened. It was the next day. I was away at the time.'

'You were? I see.' He began to write, slowly, in his notebook. 'And if you wouldn't mind telling me where you were, and when you went away.'

She was reluctant to tell him anything at all – he found it difficult to decide whether this was from bloody-mindedness or because she had something to hide. She was ill at ease, shifting under his gaze, glancing frequently at her watch, but, eventually, he drew the facts out.

Shortly before Alfred's death Nella went to visit an elderly relative, a Lynchet cousin, in Southwold. Asked if there was any particular reason for the visit, Nella sharply asked in turn why there had to be a reason. Blandly, Hunter observed that Southwold was a very pleasant place for a seaside holiday, then waited, pencil poised, while she fussed on endlessly about the relative not being at all well and Grandmother saying it would

– or rather, she corrected herself, *she* thought it would be a kindness to spend a little time with her . . .

Which went a long way to explaining Nella's attitude. A grown woman would scarcely want to admit to a stranger that she'd been ordered away, with no say in the matter at all – because that was undoubtedly what had happened.

'And then, my grandmother telephoned me the day after the accident.'

'The day after.'

'She was far too upset at the time, she couldn't be expected . . . once she had coped with the shock . . . then she had the distressing task of telling me . . . I travelled home that day . . .'

He half listened until she had talked herself into silence, then noted the name and address of the relative.

'I really can't imagine, Mr Hunter, how my presence or absence can do anything to facilitate your enquiries into Alfred's death.'

'It's surprising how all kinds of peripheral details can add to the overall picture,' Hunter said, at his most gnomic, making the kind of movement indicative of leaving. Before it came to anything, he sat down again. Keen to be rid of him, she had followed suit and was left, awkwardly, half in and half out of the big armchair.

'Do you recall, shortly before you went away, your grandmother had a visitor. A middle-aged woman, plump, very blonde –'

'Really, why you all persist in badgering me about this person . . . I have only the vaguest recollection of some common-looking woman.' Her exasperation appeared to him perfectly genuine.

'Your grandmother didn't say anything to you about her afterwards, explain who she was?'

A faint surprise rapidly passed across Nella's face – he could only presume it was at the notion of her grandmother bothering to explain anything. 'I certainly didn't concern myself. I have given it some thought since your – er – people were here. I recall I was not at all well, I'd had to come home with a migraine. And the next day I was suddenly so busy organising myself to go to Cousin Audrey's . . .'

Suddenly. 'Yes, it always takes more arranging than you expect – doing something at short notice,' he said chattily, getting up to go. 'Seeing to domestic matters, cancelling appointments – and you'd have had to let your office know you wouldn't be going in.'

She was too intent ushering him through the hall to bother to answer. 'I trust I shan't be pestered with more irrelevant enquiries. This woman can have no signifi-cance whatsoever.'

'That's something we haven't yet evaluated.'

'Do you expect to?' she asked ironically.

'Hard to say, now she's dead,' Hunter said cheer-fully.

Dora telephoned Inez. 'I've had the police round again.'

'Lucky you. Some of them are smashing. I think Sam's fallen in love with young Sergeant Collier.'

'Really? How nice. Is it reciprocated?' They gossiped for a while, then Dora said, 'There's something I think I remember, but I'm not sure if I ought to . . .'

'What is it, old love?'

Dora reminded her of their evening in the One-eyed Rat. 'It never entered my head then, and even when the police were here just now, asking. They wanted to know if anyone had means of access to Jaynie's. Well, that translates as a key, doesn't it?'

'Yes, it must.'

'It wasn't until after they'd gone, I remembered how we'd talked about Nella's accident. Somebody – at the

time it happened, I can't for the life of me think who –
said something about the big thing Jaynie made about
an arrangement – between friends . . . You don't remember, I suppose?'

'I don't know what you're bloody talking about,
darling.'

'Oh, no, I keep forgetting. You were away, panning for
gold in –'

'Oh, shut up.'

'Yes, well. As they were such chums – *then* – Jaynie
told Nella where she hid the spare key to the bungalow.'

'I can't imagine Nella tripping around there and letting herself in.'

'No, of course not. It was supposed to be for emer-
gencies.'

'In case Jaynie fell down the back steps, evening the
score, so to speak.'

'Something like that – and I don't even . . . It was just
talk that was going around at the time. But now I think
about it, it's so embarrassing. I can't say something is
true when I'm not even sure. What do you think
I should do? Should I say something to the police?'

'Well, it's a bit muddled and, I agree, awkward . . .
I don't know. Shall we think about it, Door?'

'Yes. You think, they're your pals. You decide.'

'Oh, thanks,' Inez sighed.

It was because Dora spoke to her at a time when she
was occupied, her mind on other matters, that reaction
was delayed, liked a depth charge. She sat at her kitchen
table, rather bewildered, with a sense that she might
have blundered. After a while she pulled herself
together and did what she always did in times of stress:
she went round to Mrs Hanks, collected the armadillo
and took him for a walk.

They went to the Jubilee Gardens where the ground

sloped and there were networks of up and down paths, brisk walking on the bitter day. She told him all about it: *I value your advice, old chap.*

When she had made up her mind, she went down into the town, to the police station.

Chapter Twenty-three

Inez lingered about the front yard of the police station, while the armadillo inspected everything within reach of his nose. 'I feel a bit of an ass, now,' she whispered to him. They edged a little farther, then the door opened and a big man, moving so quickly he almost collided with her, came out, side-stepped briskly. She smiled happily. 'Sheldon.'

His occupied air vanished, he looked pleased, then knowing. 'What are you and that dog doing lurking out here?'

'Waiting for you.' She had an inspiration. 'It's lunchtime. I've made a chicken and mushroom pie.'

An unmistakable longing. 'Inez, I can't think of anything . . . but . . .' The armadillo began an enthusiastic welcome at ground level.

'Of course, you're busy, I understand. But, also, there is something I'd like to talk to you about – when – when you have time.'

'It must be important, or you wouldn't be here, would you? Or you . . .' He bent down to give the armadillo a friendly ruffling. 'Tell me.'

'I've been in two minds . . . I might be falsely accusing . . .' How feeble she must sound to this nicest of men, who had put aside his haste and waited patiently in the cold, smiling encouragingly at her. 'One evening,' she said sensibly, 'I was taking the armadillo home from the One-eyed Rat. It was the night Dora told me that Jaynie was missing. On the way to Mrs Hanks' – I can't be sure – I think Nella came out of Jaynie's bungalow.'

'Did she?' He regarded her thoughtfully. 'Right. One minute.' He went back into the police station, emerged rapidly. 'OK. Take me and show me, we'll talk as we go.'

They went along Riverside where the massive old trees leaned towards the river, their stripped, bleached branches scooping over the grass like skeletal hands. They passed closed cafés, boats roped into their tarpaulin shrouds. Shuttered shops behind which lurked Toddy souvenirs. Clerehaven sleeping out of season. The hard sunlight had faded to gloom, making the day stealthy, mysterious.

Hunter said, 'You were on your way from the One-eyed Rat. So it was Monday.'

'Yes. I hadn't realised till then that no one had seen Jaynie since I saw her the Friday before.' They were climbing steadily, up from the river, skirting the Jubilee Gardens. 'I can go three or four different ways to Mrs Hanks', I just happened to choose The Avenue, no reason . . .'

She described what had happened and, when they reached the house before Jaynie's, she halted, showed him how she'd had to go into the entrance to the driveway to retrieve the armadillo. 'As I was leading him out, putting his lead on, I was partly aware of a light going on and off somewhere on my right; then I heard a gate closing – a quiet clangy sound. When I stood up and looked along the road – that was Nella walking away . . . I think.'

His gaze took in the low stone wall that ran from the driveway to the high beech hedge separating the two properties, then the ornamental fence of Jaynie's garden. They walked slowly along it towards the wrought-iron gates. Inez could hardly feel furtive in broad daylight, but she certainly felt conspicuous, although nobody lingered on such an unpleasant day, they could be seen from windows. Supposing a friend saw her: *What were you doing hanging around Jaynie's with that policeman? Oh, nothing, only shopping Nella . . .*

'It *was* dark, though, and I couldn't –'

'But the street lights were on, weren't they? And someone you are familiar with has a distinctive outline, walk . . . Their clothes, the way they wear their clothes . . . there are a dozen points of recognition you don't even take into account. Come on, Inez.'

'Well, yes. I think it was Nella. But when I asked her –'

'You asked her?'

'Yes, on the Wednesday morning. Well, not asked straight out, I didn't want her to think I'd been spying on her, so I said someone thought they'd seen her calling on Jaynie. Silly me. I should know better. She'd rather clean out the drains. Anyway, she just dismissed the idea, pretty rudely I might say, and then – I didn't know about the key.'

'Key?'

She told him about Dora's phone call, about her recollection being unreliable. 'And it's not to say that since then, Jaynie didn't move the key, put it in another hiding place.'

'And you – or Dora – have no idea where it might have been?'

'Gosh, no.'

They had looked in all the likely places people trustingly conceal spare keys – but perhaps their search had not been thorough enough. Before beginning another one, they could take a short cut, ask Jaynie's cleaning lady.

Hunter thought of the missing file and address book, of a short, busy figure trotting away in the darkness. Ms Nella had some talking to do.

'Right.' He looked at his watch. 'I should be on my

157

way to Chatfield, but it'll keep a little longer. What about this chicken and mushroom pie?'

Her cottage was warm, shadowy till she put on lamps. She left him in the sitting-room, tactfully closing the door – 'I'll be in the kitchen.' He phoned through to Clerehaven, gave instructions to the murder team to call on Jaynie's cleaning lady, then he followed Inez.

She had been baking, the kitchen worktops were lined with pies and quiches ready for the freezer. Hunter knew himself, briefly, to be in heaven. They ate at the kitchen table, the pie's golden crust fragrant and melting; potatoes and peas. The armadillo had his own bowls, one for water, one containing biscuits that looked like cardboard and which he ate with relish before curling up on Hunter's feet.

Hunter said, 'I spoke to Nella this morning. She's pretty difficult, isn't she?'

'I think she's getting worse.'

'Do you mean that?'

She considered. 'Yes. Yes, I do. Perhaps having to handle Alfred's affairs is too much for her and she can't admit it to herself. She does sound quite manic at times. And living alone doesn't suit everyone.'

'Especially in a mausoleum.'

'You think it's . . . You should have seen it when Grandmother was running the show, it was ghastly. I know it's not exactly the house beautiful but it's a dickens of an improvement. Nella's made it, well, live-able. She'd never had a say in anything until old Mrs Lynchet died, then she was quite alone. Before that there'd always been her and Alfred – and Benjamin until Alfred died – but I don't suppose he counts.'

Hunter put down his knife and fork. 'Hang on, Benjamin left years before that.'

She looked puzzled. 'No he didn't.'

'I understood he'd been gone about eight years.'

'Whatever makes you think that?'

I didn't think. Nella told me . . .

The kettle boiled. Inez got up to pour water into the cafetière; the fragrance of fresh coffee filled the room. She sat down again. 'I spoke to him just a few days before Alfred's death – a week at most. I remember thinking after the accident that at least Nella and the old girl would have a man about the place – company, support . . . you know. Although really, I can't see him ever being much of either. He always made me think of that weird poem:

'As I was going up the stair
I met a man who wasn't there.
He wasn't there again today.
I wish, I wish he'd stay away.'

'But he already had. When?' It had now become important to know. Why had he simply taken Nella's word for it? Because there was no reason for her to misrepresent the time – perhaps she hadn't, perhaps it was a momentary mental aberration; he knew it was important to find out.

Inez thought, shook her head. 'It must have been between the time I saw him and Alfred's funeral. He wasn't the sort of person you'd miss unless there was something else to remember.'

'And he wasn't at Alfred's funeral? I assume you went.'

'Oh, yes. I was there, but – um – no, Benjamin wasn't. That didn't surprise anyone – anyone who knew him, that is. He was hopeless mixing with people. He *could* have been around, somewhere, he enjoyed pottering in the garden at Ferns, but he was pretty well out of sight there. And if anyone called, he just went in the house. Faded away. That was Benjamin.'

Thoughtful, Hunter finished his pie, made no resistance to a second helping. 'But I thought you said – when

I was talking to you and Dora – that he used to go about with Alfred to all these societies and things where Alfred bored everyone rigid.'

'Oh, God, don't remind me. It was when Benjamin first came to stay with them, Alfred tried to get him involved, give him an interest – but it was no good, Benjamin was so odd and awkward. Frankly, whenever he *didn't* turn up with Alfred, everyone sighed with relief. Eventually he stopped turning up altogether. Of course, Alfred patronised Benjamin – but then he patronised everyone – and he might just have been out to add to the boredom potential. He could do that single-handed, anyway, on a good day, with a following wind.'

She left him to his thoughts while she put a raspberry gateau and creamy, crumbly Cheshire cheese and biscuits on the table. Hunter contemplated how wonderfully good food aided mental processes. He said, eventually, 'It's a fox and hedgehog thing.'

Inez searched her memory, found what she was looking for and quoted, '*The fox knows many things . . .*'

'*But the hedgehog knows one big thing.*'

'Nella's the hedgehog.'

'I think so. I think she knows something that involves Alfred, Grandmother and Benjamin.'

'She very well could, they were always secretive and odd. She was the only one who came anywhere near normal and pleasant.'

'That's not something anyone could say about her now.'

'No. That's what I mean. After Alfred's death, there were just her and Grandmother – who took over Alfred's concerns –'

'The sacred trust.'

'You said it. But she was very old and she could have begun to fail long before it was evident – to outsiders, I mean. She was so incredibly forceful, she'd make sure everything was arranged beforehand – before it was too late for her to cope. That would mean, maybe, telling Nella things she hadn't known or didn't really want to know . . .' She spoke more and more slowly while he watched her with interest.

'What is it?' he asked after a while.

She was fed up with *not* telling him things, she would tell him everything, whether it had any significance or not.

'Some time before Grandmother became really ill, incapable, I was walking up on the Stray . . .' She told him about coming upon Nella, sitting in her car; her manner so strange she had felt compelled to walk to Ferns afterwards, to see everything was all right. 'It was. I felt rather a fool. It was after that Nella began to change – not drastically, but she wasn't her ordinary self; we all put it down to her having to cope with an increasingly gaga old lady. But it was after Grandmother's death that she became noticeably different – even her appearance . . .'

She told him about the shopping orgy at Blossom's department store, Nella having her hair styled.

He said, doubtfully, 'She certainly wears terrific clothes –'

'Oh, she's outgrown Blossom's now. Buys them in London –'

'Yes, but with all due respect, Inez, I don't know what she was like before, but she's hardly . . .'

'Course she's not. But she was a *sight*. I mean it. Just take a look at the old photos in Jaynie's "research" file – if you can bear to.'

I wouldn't mind the chance. The whole lot have disappeared.

'Grandmother bullied her into looking like some ghastly overgrown 1930s moppet. It never occurred to her she could look half-way presentable.'

'Until you showed her.'

'Well, anyone would have done, she was just waiting for someone to give her a shove. She needed to be

noticeably different And she is. Increasingly confident –
read aggressive. Decisive – read domineering, need I go
on?'

Fortified by the best meal he'd had in a long time,
Hunter walked through the silent gardens of Cremorne
cursing himself. Why had nobody checked up exactly
when Benjamin went away? *He* was the one who'd
taken Nella's word for it and everyone else followed
suit. It was his fault, entirely.

He needed to give himself time for quiet thought. To
prepare himself for two questions he could not yet make
sense of at all.

Could it possibly have been Benjamin who murdered
Tracy Lyons? After all, when Queenie went to Ferns she
saw only the old lady and Nella; not the punter who
called himself John.

And if Nella knew the family secret – had Jaynie
found out, too? Was that why she had been murdered?

Inez had resolutely ignored her answering machine all
day. She knew there was a message there, she knew it
was from Nella. When the short day moved towards
evening she wrapped up warmly, collected the notes
she'd made for Nella, said to the armadillo, 'Come on,
old chap, we'll take you home and drop these off on the
way.'

Chapter Twenty-four

The thought came to Inez of how many times she had walked between the dark conifers, the trees unchanging season by season, year in, year out, growing more dense and obscuring.

Ferns itself stood offset at the end of the drive; slightly back from it and to the side there was the large double garage-cum-workshop. Inez had been in there on one or two previous occasions. She knew the workbench lining one side, was fascinated by the neatly laid out tools, equipment arranged, hanging on precisely labelled boards. An obsessive tidiness – nothing to do with Nella, she left all practicalities to the handyman – that made Inez's garage look as if an orgy had taken place.

In the gathering dusk, the brooding silence, the sound of voices carried, indistinct. There was a light on in the garage; the double doors stood open. *Good God, Nella's got a man in there.* Stricken by the middle-class terror of being suspected of eavesdropping, Inez approached, calling, 'Hallo – Nella – it's me, Inez.' The armadillo, too quick for her, scuttled forward to investigate and was at once swallowed into the garage. Then Nella, storming – or so it appeared – pulling the door to behind her. 'Inez, I'm extremely occupied. What are you doing here?' She was agitated to the point of panting, her voice shrill.

Uncomprehending, embarrassed, Inez found herself burbling, 'You wanted – these – Hatchcliffe Hall . . .', thrust the papers into Nella's hand and then retreated.

The door slipped Nella's grasp. Through the widening gap the glimpse of a figure; then a low, vicious voice – 'Gerroff . . .'

A yelp, and the armadillo shot out, streaking down the drive. Inez turned on a reflex to follow, thinking as she marched away, poor little armadillo, he doesn't mean any harm.

She glanced back. Nella clutched the door, closing herself behind it, her face hanging formless and pale in the fading evening, like an unlit pumpkin mask.

'Come on, old chap, let's take you home.' Inez picked him up, walked on, while he pressed himself against the soft comfort of her body.

Beyond the automatic action and words lay a limitless and blighted desert of disbelief.

She had little recollection of returning him to Mrs Hanks, of walking back to Cremorne. Then she realised she was running down her front path, key stabbing and fumbling at the door, glancing back over her shoulder. Her neighbours' houses were in darkness; she had been many times here alone, conscious of the obscure location, the sheltering walls, the security lights – but she never remembered being so afraid in all her life.

She could not stay in her own house, vulnerable, confused beyond thought. She grabbed her handbag, let herself out of the side door into her garage, head turning constantly, seeking for the least movement in the surrounding dark.

She roared out of Cremorne and was almost at Sam's before she remembered he was away on a course. Where? Dora. Comforting Dora who would not think her mad. John, Dora's husband, safe, rock solid –

She bounced along the unmade road, left her car unlocked, let herself in through the five bar gate and sprinted up the drive. For an instant she deliberately blanked out the perception that there were no welcoming lights: hall, sitting-room – *anywhere*. The porch light came on automatically, blinding her. No sound from within, no footsteps.

She was on her way back down the drive, half walking, half running, when she caught the flash of lights from the next house. She was at the drive entrance when Dora's neighbour drove out, slowed, let her window down. 'Oh, Inez, are you looking for Dora? You don't know. Didn't she phone?'

I don't know anything. The only message I've had was from Nella Lynchet who is probably out of her mind.

Or am I?

Dora's neighbour was talking, telling her – 'Poor dear. Her youngest daughter – you know, Emma. She's had a miscarriage . . .'

Oh, no. The longed-for grandchild . . . oh, no . . . She said the right things, somehow, sympathy briefly displacing everything else. Of course Emma would want her mother and father to be with her, of course.

'Sorry, Inez, awful shock for you, too. But I must dash, I'm late –'

'Yes, yes, thanks for telling . . . Bye.'

Then she was alone, on the unmade road with the trees sighing and the concealing bushes and the grass verges where no footfall would sound.

Into her sense of self-preservation, her conviction she was in danger, came the thought that she was drawing danger to friends. She needed to be somewhere safe and impersonal, where there would be lights and the company of people.

The market square. She sat in her car – for how long she had no idea. Her confusion didn't clear, but it pointed direction: she couldn't stay there, she had to go somewhere.

There was only one place.

An accident caused a traffic tailback on the A54, and

there were road delays in Chatfield. It was six thirty by the time she walked into Chatfield subdivisional headquarters.

'I'm sorry, DCI Hunter isn't in,' the young constable at the desk informed her.

'No, he'll have gone home,' Inez said sensibly.

'Can anyone else help?'

I doubt it very much. I can trust my madness only to him. 'No, thank you, I'll – er – yes. Goodnight.' If he had gone home, where was that? She had no idea. She knew no one would give her his address, even if she banged on the counter and threatened to have a fit. She did not even have a number where she could reach him, apart from his official one.

Her car was tucked into a corner of the police car park and no one seemed to mind about it being there. She left it and wandered away. It was a reasonably busy part of town, emptying after the day's business, filling with pleasure seekers. She paused outside a café, said to herself, no, dammit, I need something stronger, walked on until she found a respectable-looking pub. She had some wine and, surprisingly hungry, a sandwich. She sat there for a long time, warmed by the comings and goings of people intent on an evening's enjoyment. A flashy, middle-aged man tried to pick her up. She left, wandered about for a while, still with no idea of what to do, then went back to the car park and got into her car.

She switched the radio on and sat, not listening. After a while, the cold got to her; she pulled a travelling rug from the back seat and wriggled herself into it.

She woke from a terrified dream. Heavy, menacing footsteps pursued her, drawing ever closer. She was slowing, slowing, nearing paralysis . . .

She opened bleary eyes; she was entrapped in the rug,

frozen, stiff-limbed. And Hunter was knocking on the car window.

She opened the door, half fell out, her legs rigid. He hauled her up, supported her, began to unwind her from the rug. She heard her voice rushing on: 'Last night – I know it's silly – but what happened – I didn't feel safe – anywhere. After.'

'All right, take it easy. Let's lock your car.'

'After Ferns –'

'You've been at Ferns?'

'That's what I'm trying to tell you.' Her voice rose.

'Yes, steady . . .'

She was talking, being soothed, led into the police station. Corridors, doors; people. If they looked at her oddly she had no time to notice, or care. 'It was yesterday.'

'Yes, yes. What time, Inez?'

'Does the sodding time matter?' Loud again. 'Oh, I'm sorry.'

'Never mind. Sit down –'

'Time? Time . . . Early evening, getting dark.' She sat down, immediately stood up again. 'I saw him, I saw him. He's *dead*.'

'Who is? Who did you see?'

'I know his voice – but – a beard . . . He always hated dogs. Nella pushed me out of the way –'

'Who did you see?'

She could not look at him, turned her face away, whispered.

'Inez, you've got confused. You mean Benjamin, don't you?'

She shouted, 'No, I don't, I don't!'

He put his arms around her, held her, shaking.

She said, 'I'm sorry, Sheldon. But he was there. At Ferns. Alfred.'

Chapter Twenty-five

It was extraordinary how such a commonplace activity as drinking tea restored order. Somebody – an unregistered, reassuringly physical presence – had brought in the tray, set it down on Hunter's desk.

She had a cup in her hand and was recounting, with some degree of sanity, what had occurred at Ferns.

'I was so sure I was in danger, that he'd follow me and find me. So I came here, to see you –'

'You've been here all night?'

'Yes. I couldn't think what to do when you weren't here. I just fell asleep.'

'I *was* here, but I had to go back to Clerehaven yesterday, early evening. I was at Ferns. Because Nella had telephoned the Clerehaven police –'

She could feel only relief at this confirmation of something terribly awry.

'– she said that Benjamin Wright had suddenly turned up. He threatened her life. She killed him in self-defence.'

This conundrum had begun, for Hunter, on the evening of the previous day. A telephone call from Clerehaven reported the bare details: Miss Nella Lynchet had killed, in self-defence, an intruder who was threatening her life.

In view of her confession, Nella was arrested and cautioned. By the time Hunter got to Ferns, in the wake of all the scene of crime paraphernalia, she had been taken to Clerehaven police station where she had been interviewed on tape; her account of events was now a matter of record. It did not entirely make sense, in fact, what she did say was so disjointed and contradictory Hunter was in a quandary about whether to call in medical attention. But he persevered and eventually worked out a sequence.

Benjamin Wright, a one-time house-guest, had turned up without any warning as she was putting her car away in the garage. When she stepped out of the car he was there, obviously in a stressed condition. He began to make wild accusations which she did not understand. She tried to soothe him but, unable to do so, eventually threatened to call the police. He then said he would kill her as he had killed 'that woman' and got hold of her. She wrestled with him, managed to distract his attention, which gave her time to snatch up the nearest object from the workbench beside her – a four-pound lump hammer. She struck him with it and he fell to the ground instantly. She waited, too shocked to do anything; she could not bring herself to touch him but after a while, as he did not move and she could not see him breathing, she realised he was dead. She went into the house, became faint and sat down, she had no idea how long for. She then felt compelled to take off her clothes, feeling 'soiled'. She went upstairs and made a complete change. After that she telephoned Clerehaven police.

Hunter, accompanied by Annette, went gently but thoroughly through her statement. Nella was composed, subdued and had the faintly distant manner he had seen so often in people in shock. He asked her several times about Benjamin's accusations; every time she said she didn't know what they were, she couldn't understand them. Was he speaking English? Yes. Was he incoherent? Yes. Could she not distinguish any words at all? Not one.

When she was asked who he meant by 'that woman' she said she had no idea.

She had struggled with him? Yes. How did she account for the fact that the clothes she had removed showed no signs of damage, no tears, missing buttons etc? She could not.

She claimed to have snatched up the hammer from the workbench beside her but the body was found near the garage door, on the side opposite the workbench, and the blow was to the back of the head. She was confused, their struggle had carried them back and forth.

He would form a clearer picture when he had the scene of crime report and when the search of Ferns had been completed. Meanwhile, in the face of Inez's evidence, more contradictions and inaccuracies surfaced.

At no time had Nella mentioned anyone had called whilst 'Benjamin' was with her.

She had said that once she had gone into the house she had not returned to the garage. But why were the papers Inez had delivered to her not found in the garage?

'Inez, you gave her these papers? Put them in her hands?'

'Yes.'

'How many? A lot?'

'Oh, no. Three sheets of biog, one of the suggested programme.'

'And she didn't go at once into the house with them? She went back into the garage, you said. And closed the door.'

'Yes. She was doing that when I looked back.'

It was impossible to credit that after struggling for her life, committing an act of unparalleled violence, Nella had tidily picked up the scattered papers and taken them away. Inez didn't ask why he wanted to know; she sat pale and tired and bemused, drinking her tea in a quietly trustful way. No harm could come to her here.

'I know these details might seem unimportant, but I promise you they're not, they could be vital. I'd like you to make a statement about everything that happened at Ferns, Annette or Collier will help you through it.'

She nodded. 'OK. Now?'

'We'll go down to Clerehaven and see to it there. For the moment, I'd like you to think back.' She pulled a wry face: *I'd rather not.* 'Can you be sure there was only one man in the garage?'

She looked uncertain. 'Not absolutely. It's big . . . and it was shadowy, dark corners . . .'

'Both the doors were open?'

'Yes, but I called out before I reached them and as soon as Nella appeared she pulled one of the doors closed behind her.'

'Was there a light on?'

'No . . . no, I'm sure not.'

Open doors and no interior light squared with Nella's claim that she had reversed into the garage, using her reversing lights, and been accosted as she got out of her car.

'So there could have been another man there – someone you couldn't see.'

'Well, if there was he had nothing to say for himself. As I got near I heard only two voices. I couldn't make out what they were saying but I knew one was Nella's, the other, a man's.'

'You didn't recognise it then as Alfred's?'

'No,' she said unhappily. 'I didn't because – obviously – it wasn't what I expected to hear. But there was something . . . and then he shouted at the armadillo . . . Then I couldn't believe my ears. And he kicked him. Alfred would, I've seen him do it in the past, he couldn't bear dogs anywhere near him. Besides, I just somehow *knew* there were only two people there. Don't ask me how.'

'Right. Now I'm going to tell you something. Probably

171

I shouldn't, but I trust you. And I have a very special reason.'

She smiled, gave a small shrug, as if to say *What next?*

'Nella claims that man was Benjamin. You say he was Alfred. I'm going to tell you something about Alfred's death . . .'

He kept it brief, because he was dealing in the barest essentials and because she had suffered a shock and must shortly endure another.

She stared at him wordlessly for a while, then said, 'How could she – how could anyone – do such a dreadful thing?'

'I think I know why, but I have to be sure. In the meantime, will you rely on my judgement?'

'There's damn all else I can rely on,' she said wearily.

'OK. It's a great deal to ask of you, but in view of what I've just told you, you'll understand why. Will you identify the man Nella claims is Benjamin?'

She stood close to him, to the reassurance of his calm, warmed by his humanity. He prepared her: 'Sometimes people look so different in death it's difficult to recognise them. Don't be upset if you can't be sure.'

'I know.' Her face had lost all its colour. Her hand touched his, he held it, icily cold. She said. 'All right.'

The attendant rolled the body out. She looked steadily, then swallowed, whispered, 'Yes, yes, it is.'

'Right. Come along.'

An incident room had been set up overnight in Clerehaven police station. Hunter had commandeered a cubby hole of an office; at least it was private. He produced a bottle of whisky and two glasses. 'Here. Medicinal. You need it.'

He put the glass securely into her shaking hand. After some sips she began to talk, hesitant but composed. 'He must have had some identification on him. Driving licence whatever.'

'Nothing. Banknotes in his wallet. No credit cards, not a scrap of anything in writing to say who he was or where he came from.'

'Isn't that the sort of thing you'd find odd?'

'It happens more often than you'd think. People have their own reasons for remaining anonymous. If he'd had a fatal accident – road, train – before he got to Clere-haven, it would have been virtually impossible to find out who he was. So far there's only you to say he's Alfred. You are sure?'

'He's different – older. Of course. And the beard changes – him. He had – it was a childhood accident, I believe – a white scar on his left temple. You noticed it?'

'Yes.'

'I'll tell you, Sheldon, I'm sure. That is Alfred, not Benjamin.'

Chapter Twenty-six

•

Inez had seldom had occasion to enter Clerehaven police station; she began to feel, during the endless day, that she would never get out of it.

James Collier helped her with her statement; he was friendly and kind and she marvelled at his patience. It was early afternoon when at last they finished. 'You must be hungry,' he said. Surprisingly, she was. 'The canteen's not cordon bleu, but it's good solid food, that's what you need.'

'How's Nella?'

His only previous acquaintance with Nella being unpleasant and humiliating, he was not kindly disposed to her. But he had his orders. 'She seems to be coping. She isn't an easy person, is she?'

Inez smiled wryly. 'Not a characteristic the Lynchets are noted for. She's in a frightful situation, and she doesn't have any relatives, not accessible, anyway . . .'

'You can see her, if you'd like to.'

'Well . . . has anyone? Friends . . .'

He shook his head.

'No, there aren't many of those. Yes, all right. For all the good I'll be.'

'Come and have something to eat first. Then have a word with Mr Hunter.'

Substantial, if basic, food, made her feel more capable of coping with whatever the day might throw at her. She would far rather just go home, even though there were friendly faces around her here: James, Annette, Hunter;

but Nella, embattled and alone, was on her conscience.

James took her through some corridors, where there
seemed to be a lot of activity – change of shift, he told
her. 'If you'll just hang on I'll find – ah, here he is.' He
murmured something unheard to Hunter and at once
disappeared.

Hunter had an air of preoccupation which, in view of
everything that was happening, he could scarcely be
expected to put aside. He said, 'James says you're kind
enough to have a talk to Nella.'

Then he did it bloody quickly, unless some kind of
ESP operates here. It probably does, she thought resign-
edly. 'It's just that I can't help feeling sorry . . .'

'Yes, come on, I'll take you.' As they walked down yet
another corridor, he said, 'You remember you told me
you saw Benjamin shortly before Alfred's death.'

'Yes.'

'Well, have I lost my place somewhere? I thought that
before that you told me Benjamin had just stopped
going around, socially, dropped out – no one saw him.
But you did – so where was it?'

'On his evening walk; depending on the time of year,
he always went out at dusk. Then, you see, there were
few people about, they were home having drinks or
supper or watching telly. And he never strayed from
High Town, where it's always quiet. I used to come
across him sometimes because I'm out and about at all
times with the armadillo.'

'So he stuck to the same area?'

'He stuck to the same route. That's the way it seemed
to me.'

'He was always alone?'

'Very occasionally Alfred was with him. Usually just
by himself, though.'

'And that evening, that last evening, you spoke to
him?'

'Only in passing, just hallo, nice-evening, terrible-evening. He always had more to say to the armadillo, patting him and muttering something, I've no idea what . . .'

Always dusk, always round High Town. So when he went out on his last walk, there were a few people who knew exactly where he would be.

Nella's face was putty-coloured, her manner grand – unhurried, queenly movements; but she had an air that hinted she had mislaid something and couldn't think what it was.

In the old-fashioned police station, considerable effort had gone into making the interview room less institutionalised. It was decorated in pastel colours, with matching curtains. They sat in easy chairs before a low table, a young WPC positioned on a chair by the door.

Hunter's advice to Inez had been to go straight out – tell Nella she had recognised Alfred. Inez, while appreciating the value of shock tactics, found this was something she could not do. She didn't know whether it was because her nerve failed or because she felt sorry for Nella. She simply said the first thing that came into her head. 'Is there something you'd like to talk about? In the past, I've helped you whenever I could. I'd like to now, if you'd let me, now that you're in trouble.'

'Trouble?' A patronising smile, a studied, dismissive gesture of the hand. 'If I were in the least trouble, I can't imagine what you could do. My solicitor, Mr Jelks, will instruct a QC of the highest possible calibre to act in my defence – which is that in the act of defending my life I have ridded society of a murderer.'

'Well, I suppose that's one –'

'I have no intention of asking for preferential treatment because of who I am, the law must take its course, I shall pay any penalty it requires. With my faith in

British justice I know I will receive a fair trial. I shall, of course, shrink from the inevitable vulgar interest . . .'

No, you won't, you'll love it, Inez thought wildly.

While Nella continued to amplify her future role, Inez sat bemused by the notion that Nella had moved from her cherished position of being in control of Alfred's fiction to writing a part in it for herself. Was it shock? Hunter had told her: 'The way to cope with shock is to square up to reality.' She should have followed his advice in the first place. She said, kindly but positively, 'Nella, it was Alfred. In the garage at Ferns. I saw him. I heard his voice.'

Nella stared at her coldly. 'No, you're mistaken, that's absurd. You mustn't say such things.'

'Both the garage doors were open as I came up the drive, I heard −'

'I'd forgotten you were there − which shows the severity of the trauma I've suffered. It is extremely cruel of you to take advantage of me in this way.'

'I'm not, but I know −'

'I'm surprised. Even with your love of posturing and exaggeration, I wouldn't have believed you would go to such lengths to draw attention to yourself.'

'Draw . . . Look here −'

'No, you look. I will not tolerate your going around saying such wicked things. It's doubtful anyone will listen to you, it's your word against mine, and I command considerably more respect than you. But I warn you, I will not hesitate to take legal action should you persist in this fantasy.'

Momentarily speechless, Inez recognised the tactic: browbeat, intimidate; she recognised the rigid, intense manner; recognised in the loud, cultured voice the hectoring tones of Grandmother Lynchet. It was unnerving: Nella's short dumpy body possessed by the merciless spirit of a tall, gaunt old woman. She said, with gentle desperation, 'Nella, I don't know why you're attacking

177

me like this, but you must stop. You're confused, under-
standably, by what's happened –'

'You're the last person qualified to patronise me, Inez.
I behaved with courage in a dangerous situation that
was not of my own making. If that woman hadn't been
so reckless and self-centred –'

'That woman. You mean Jaynie –'

'She brought it all on herself. It was she who lured
Benjamin from – wherever he was – I don't know –'

'*Benjamin.* It wasn't –'

'If she hadn't pried into our affairs, and put me in
peril –'

Has she really just said 'peril'? Am I going mad?

'– she was about to unmask him as the murderer of
some prostitute in the past. He told me, he told me all
about it, before he – he attacked me. He had always been
unbalanced – well, you can testify to that –'

'I am not doing any testifying for –'

'– and living as he has been these last few years, an
awful life, feckless, drinking, gambling, his character
deteriorated completely.'

'I thought you'd lost contact with him?'

'What?' Nella looked at her with the air of abstraction
that had been noticeable earlier.

'How could Jaynie possibly know that he'd com-
mitted murder years ago?'

'She found out – her *research*. And she threatened to
tell the police. I've said that already, haven't I? Do try
and follow, Inez.'

'But how could *she* know? She wasn't a – a detective.'
She wasn't even very bright.

'She thought she was, prying and ferreting. She dug
up all sorts of things about people, you were fortunate
she didn't turn her attention on you –'

'The only sense that makes is that there was something for her to dig up – that Benjamin – that Benjamin
really *did* murder someone.'

'Of course, he was always jealous of Alfred.' Nella

spoke confidentially. 'In spite of Alfred doing what he could to help. Resented his talent, his success, well, you know that only too well.'

Why did Nella keep trying to enlist her support?

At the moment she asked herself that, Nella looked away. But not before her sideways glance revealed an instant's unmistakable slyness, repellent and baffling because there was something specific in that slyness – it came to her suddenly; Hunter's words over lunch at Cremorne: *The hedgehog knows one big thing.*

Not abstraction. Calculation.

She said quietly, 'You're not talking about Benjamin – you're talking about Alfred. You've misidentified him – just as your grandmother did, just as deliberately.'

Nella's eyes narrowed, she drew in a hissing breath. 'How dare you say such vile things. You don't imagine anyone's going to take account of your maunderings? Everyone knows you make things up.'

'I have no possible reason for making this up. You have. To save the reputation of the Lynchets. To save Alfred's reputation.'

Nella said loudly, 'I insist you leave now. You are behaving like a fishwife, screaming insults –'

'No, if there's any screaming it's going on inside your head.' It was true, Nella would hear only what she wished to hear. 'Listen.' She spoke firmly. 'I saw Alfred. I saw his body, I recognised him. I identified him.'

'Don't be ridiculous. *Recognised.* How could you? He'd grown a beard.'

Inez sat for a moment, then found her voice. 'Do you know what you've just said? You've admitted it was Alfred. Nella, you're in a desperate situation, but if you go on telling lies –'

Nella stood with unexpected speed, slapped Inez across the face with her right hand, punched her in the chest with her left. The WPC was there, wrestling her back. Inez sat dazed. Nella shouted, 'Alfred's reputation

---

is secure. Nothing, no one, can take it away. It is *his* work – *his* work – there is no one . . .'

The room suddenly filled with people. Inez put her hand to her stinging cheek. In a sickening insight she saw the answer to the whole conundrum, but she was trying to keep her head before the onslaught of too many improbabilities. Whatever she understood at that moment disappeared, at once, into confusion.

'All right?' Hunter said.

He had his arms securely round her. It was only comfort but she really did not wish to be anywhere else. All in the course of duty for him, but nevertheless, a private space. 'Yes. She packed quite a punch.'

'You ladylike types are all the same when it comes to putting the boot in.'

'Well, you'd know.' She moved reluctantly away. 'I was your stalking horse, wasn't I?'

He looked apologetic. 'I'm sorry, I never thought she'd set about you.'

'Oh, I don't blame you. I suppose you have to use any means you can to get at the truth. Sheldon, there was a moment when she really spooked me. She could have *been* Grandmother Lynchet . . . What the hell is going on with her?'

'Don't trouble yourself, Inez. We'll get it sorted.'

'Yes, I suppose you will. For one minute there I thought I had.'

But she couldn't, she didn't know enough.

Neither did he, yet.

Chapter Twenty-seven

Nella had been told – if she had taken it in – that she could be held for only twenty-four hours, and then must be released, unless she was charged or there was any reason for her to be held in custody any longer. Hunter was confident that he had so many reasons the Superintendent would have no trouble in granting a twelve-hour extension. That still left much ground to be covered, detail to be verified, and, ultimately, he would get nowhere without hard evidence.

The duty officer authorised a search of Ferns and the team soon came up with something for Hunter to work on. DC Darrow was a keen young man with an accountancy degree; it was said of him there was nothing he liked more than being let loose to count things. From Ferns he telephoned Hunter, who was in conference about the next step in an investigation of accumulating complexity.

'Well. Is there? Now, there's a thing,' Hunter said. He knew his man and his particular expertise. 'As far back as the records you've found there? But it could pre-date those. Yes . . . I don't anticipate any trouble getting a warrant to look at her bank account, there's more than enough dodgy business going on here, her statement leaks like an old man's bladder. So, get along to wherever? Right. See how long that's been going on. OK. Benjamin Wright's address. Good. Where did you find it? Did you? Bingo, I'd say. No . . . we need someone of our own there, God knows what might turn up. Send Collier, DS Walker to go with him.'

He told his colleagues the substance of Darrow's call. 'Ms Lynchet's got a lot of fast talking to do. Her solicitor should be surfacing by now . . .' He had already been summoned, they would not interview Nella without him, having always to be aware of how any situation would look when it came to court. Ms Nella Lynchet, it was becoming obvious, was going to give them hell whatever happened; the important thing was to be in the right square whatever move she made.

Hunter and Annette confronted Nella again. Hunter had an assortment of papers on the table before him; mostly, they were no more than props, but invaluable for allowing considered pauses, searching looks, and the lengthy taking of indecipherable notes.

'During the time Mrs Jaynie Turner was missing, before her body was found, did you go to her bungalow?'

Nella appeared composed, but her eyes kept watchfully on the move – which said to Hunter that she was ready for anyone creeping up on her. 'Why on earth should I?'

'And did you let yourself in?'

'How on earth could I do that?'

'Will you answer the question, Miss Lynchet?'

'Of course I didn't. Preposterous.'

From a folder Hunter produced a see-through plastic wallet and laid it on the table before Nella. It contained a key. Her eyes flickered over it and away.

'Do you recognise this, Miss Lynchet?'

'No.'

'Would you look at it, please?'

'I have. Oh, very well.' Her glance skimmed.

Annette would never have believed a key could be flamboyant. This one was. It was attached to two rings, one an ornate gilt, the other diamanté, from which dangled a miniature gilt poodle with a diamanté collar. No one who had seen it could possibly forget it. Hunter asked again if Nella recognised it, received the same reply.

'I understand that you knew where Mrs Turner kept her spare front door key.'

'Do you? From whom?' she said strenuously and went on without waiting for a reply, 'If you use malicious gossip as a basis for your investigations, then it's not surprising –'

'Did you know, Miss Lynchet?'

'Certainly not.'

'Right. In the front porch of Mrs Turner's bungalow, there's a miniature – er – windmill. The roof of it is a pot with foliage in. If you lifted the pot out –'

'I did no such thing, it wasn't –' She stopped abruptly.

'Wasn't what?'

'It wasn't any business of mine where the woman kept her key.'

'Oh, did I say she kept it there?'

'Yes, you did.' Leaning forward, she tapped the table for emphasis. Sure of herself. 'And if you're trying to say I took it from that ridiculous object, then that is utterly untrue and something you could not prove to be so in a million years.'

'Of course I couldn't,' he said reassuringly, with an irony she would never fathom. Because the key had not been there, in that most obvious of places. Just a short distance, at the edge of the lawn, stood a lurid collection of garden ornaments, amongst them a small pig of such subdued colour it was a wonder no one had noticed it before. It was backed into a shrub, lifting its snout to reveal a partly opened mouth with nothing in it. 'What about its arse,' someone said, picking it up, and discovering, to the crudest possible hilarity, a well-disguised trapdoor beneath its tail. If the daily woman had not told them where to look, they would have been a long time finding it.

But there were no fingerprints on the key. There was no doubt Nella had used it to gain entry, just as there was no way he could prove she had set aside her dignity and rifled a pig's bum. Even so, there was some obscure satisfaction in the thought.

He took her through it again, at a quickened pace; she was adamant, unassailable.

'So you categorically deny you visited Mrs Turner's bungalow and let yourself in.'

'Absolutely.'

'We have a witness.'

'Impossible. Who could have seen me so late, in the dark?'

'Was it late, and dark, Miss Lynchet?' he asked softly.

Her solicitor, Mr Arthur Jelks, leaned forward. Mr Jelks – the haplessly bullied Lynchet family solicitor who had too often been summoned to Ferns, to endure parsimonious dinners in the frigid dining-room, being patronised, instructed, fed tiny portions of stodge and the smallest possible quantities of excellent wine. Nothing in his life, in the blameless, long tradition of his firm, could have prepared him for this. He did his best.

Hunter and Annette watched as he whispered to Nella. She stared stonily ahead, her lips set in a grim line.

'Well, Miss Lynchet?' Hunter asked.

Mr Jelks inclined timidly towards her once more, whispered. Nella recited acidly, 'I am not compelled to answer your questions. I have a right to remain silent.'

Hunter sighed. 'Very well. A search of your house has revealed –'

'Search?' She glared at him. It was barely supportable: the thought of Ferns – haven, fortress, fastness of gentility – now despoiled, besieged by teeming police, media, the vulgar public. The news that its interior was now open to the gaze of officialdom brought her close to rage. 'What do you mean? How dare you? My house . . .' She turned upon the shrinking Jelks. 'What are you going to do about this?'

Hunter replied for him, 'Under section 32 of PACE we are entitled to enter and search the premises where you were arrested –'

'I can hardly believe I have to point out to you that the *crime* took place in the garage. Your search should be confined to –'

'– for evidence relating to the offence for which you have been arrested,' Hunter concluded inexorably.

She made a sound of exasperation, sat staring into a furious distance, retrieved her hauteur. 'In that case, it was fortunate I had the foresight to lock everything up. I always lock the desk and filing cabinets when I leave the house, or when there are strangers about, ever since that dreadful woman took advantage of my good nature. I have valuable papers in my keeping, Alfred's first plot outlines – goodness knows their worth, typed on his old portable Remington, which belonged to my parents . . .'

Hunter let her continue, talking herself into a refuge out of which he could disastrously spring her. He excused himself abruptly, left the room, an unspoken message to Annette.

Annette waited while Mr Jelks held a short, whispered conversation with Nella, then said, 'I'm afraid you don't understand, Miss Lynchet.'

Nella had demolished her once, she ordered her solicitor to do it this time. 'Tell this person that I have no intention of giving my permission for my family effects to be inspected, mauled over.'

Mr Jelks, increasingly hunted, opened his mouth. Before he could speak, Annette cut in. 'What is meant by search is the entire contents of the house. It isn't a question of permission.'

Nella drew breath, visibly fought for control; when she spoke her voice was shrill. 'You mean you *broke* in – like vandals – you broke into my desk, files – committing criminal damage –'

'There has been no damage. If there has been, I can assure you we will see that you are fully reimbursed.'

Hunter returned; Nella directed a headlong tirade at him. He was reminded again that for all her arrogance, she could have been any one of the back-yard Amazons who had clouted their way through his childhood. The comparison would have mortified her. 'It would seem that once incarcerated I have no rights. I am treated like a common felon, you break into my home, allow me *on your own premises* to be assaulted by a member of the public –'

'As I understand it, the assault was carried out by you.'

'I should have foreseen she would worm her way into your confidence, passing herself off as a friend. *Friend.* That you could give any credit at all to this ghoulish claim of hers to recognise . . . I can't even speak of it. She is completely unscrupulous, anything to draw attention to herself, but you couldn't be expected to know that. She provoked me, intentionally . . .'

Annette sat staring. She had come across people like Nella – in such a muddle of cunning, naivety and insolence it was scarcely possible to distinguish truth from play-acting. At no time would she have been a match for Hunter, certainly not shocked, angry, and disoriented by her surroundings; but no one, Annette could truly say, had ever put up such a bravura performance.

Annette was working in accordance with Hunter's battle plan, which went simply: *Just when she's settled into a run about nothing – strike.* 'Why did you not tell us before that Mrs Bryant called on you last night?'

Nella gave this some consideration, spoke helplessly to Hunter. 'There are gaps in my memory. It had gone out of my head completely. Now that you remind me, I recall it, but I've suffered such shock –'

'Undoubtedly, having the brother you believed dead suddenly walk in on you.'

She had begun to relax, now she straightened: come what may, she would wield her superiority. 'This is preposterous, this insistence on something so . . . You seem incapable of understanding, Mr Hunter, I am the only person qualified to recognise my brother. How many times must I say it, Alfred was killed five years –'

'No, Benjamin died in that hit and run. That's what Alfred admitted to you last night, and you just won't accept it, will you? Your grandmother planned it. Your grandmother arranged false eye witness evidence. Your grandmother identified the body as Alfred's. It was Alfred who went out at dusk and ran Benjamin down, but your grandmother told him to do it – and he always obeyed her. Besides he didn't have much choice, did he? And Benjamin had served his purpose.'

Mr Jelks made a move towards Nella; she hissed, 'Keep quiet.' She had fastened upon Hunter, listening, watching, with a concentration so intense it was like another presence in the room.

Hunter was silent. Nella said harshly, 'I don't know what you mean.'

'His car would show signs of damage, but all he had to do was put as much distance as he could between himself and Clerehaven. Nobody would be looking for it, anyway. How did your grandmother explain its absence to you – when you got back from Southwold?' Hunter asked the question casually, looking down and making a note.

Annette said, 'Mrs Bryant gave you some papers last night, they contained information you had specifically requested from her.'

'Information? Requested?' Confused, she looked from Annette to Hunter.

He said, 'What *did* your grandmother tell you had become of Alfred's car?'

'While I was away he'd taken it in for some minor repairs, our local garage.' She was guarded, looking for a trap and, he was sure, genuinely attempting to remember.

'But didn't you go and collect it, when it was ready?'

'Oh, no. Grandmother was far too upset – she didn't want any – she instructed the garage to sell it –'

An unexpectedly genuine note, the ineffectual, obedient Nella, doing what Grandmother said; it was not altogether surprising that this prompted a return of confidence; whatever relevance Alfred's car might have had was Grandmother's responsibility. When Hunter asked for the name of the garage she said airily she had no idea.

'Presumably you have one you use regularly.'

'I don't know who Grandmother made the arrangement with.'

'We can check,' Annette said.

'Oh, well, it might have been Cranwell's, on the Chester road.'

'Now, this information you requested from Mrs Bryant –' Annette began.

'I have no idea what you're talking about. Something Inez made up, no doubt, she's notoriously unreliable.'

'We have your message on her answering machine.'

Nella said nothing.

'It concerned the performance poet at Hatchcliffe Hall.'

Nella put her hand to her brow, took her time. 'Oh, *that*. I *think* I remember that. Yes, yes . . . You see, I have so many engagements, normally I'm extremely organised. Only last week I was asked –'

Annette said, 'When she called on you at Ferns, she gave you four sheets of A4 paper.'

'Did she?'

'Yes. They were found in the hallway of the house, on the table beside the telephone. How did they get there?'

Nella made a small, defenceless gesture, directed at Hunter. 'I can't think . . . I suppose, I must . . . I could scarcely be expected to recall details after such a horrific episode.'

Annette persisted. 'You suppose you must – what, Miss Lynchet? Have taken them into the house and put them there yourself?'

She shrugged.

Hunter said, 'After this, as you say, horrific episode – during which time you could hardly have been hanging on to these papers – are you asking us to believe you collected them together, took them into the house?'

'I don't know.' Her voice rose. 'I am becoming increasing stressed by your badgering. You are trying to trap me into saying something – something –'

Hunter said, 'You'll be familiar with the large file Mrs Turner called her research.'

She struggled with the change of focus. 'What?'

'It was well known amongst your friends and acquaintances that a section of it contained a considerable amount of information about your family. There were several occasions when Mrs Turner would refer to –'

'I am not responsible for that woman's behaviour.'

'The material concerning your family is missing from the file.'

'I know nothing about it.'

'You know nothing about the file? Or nothing about it being missing?'

She was silent; her hands, very small, plump, beautifully manicured, were locked rigidly together.

'Please answer, Miss Lynchet.'

Mr Jelks inclined towards her, shrank back when she glared at him, repeated, 'I know nothing about it.'

'Then how do you account for the fact that it has been found in the filing cabinet in your study?' He waited. She could have been deaf, or somewhere else. 'It contains the name and address of Benjamin Wright.'

Chapter Twenty-eight

The drive from Cheshire to Lincolnshire took Collier and DS Walker three hours; it was late morning by the time they arrived at the Brite Caravan Park. Egerton CID's immediate reaction when Collier had telephoned earlier was now apparent – 'Shite Caravan Park, you mean. If you want someone there chances are so will everyone else. What's he done?'

'We're not sure yet if he's there.'

'They often aren't. Drugs, drink. They do the really vicious stuff off the premises; anything to stop us nosing around. There's a permanent petition hereabouts to get the place closed, nobody wants it on their doorstep.'

In a desolate landscape of stunted trees and sparse habitation, it could scarcely be said to be on anyone's doorstep, but no one sane would want it within miles. An overgrown line of cypresses guarded its perimeter; even without that it was a place where people could come and go without being noticed, swallowed from one dimension to another – miles of featureless existence into a black hole of anonymity.

There was some apparent order, here and there, in enclaves of large, garish caravans with absurd awnings, areas of decking, statuary – for Collier, Jaynie's tasteless garden was brought forcibly to mind. Round the periphery, amongst the rubbish and broken-down cars, minuscule dilapidated boxes on wheels with filthy windows and sagging curtains, Rottweilers snarled on chains.

It wasn't a travellers' site; these caravans never travelled anywhere. The people did – carried by tides of misfortune, they washed up here as detritus. It was a place, not only without hope, but of the menace that replaced the end of hope.

Collier's opposite number in Egerton CID, DS Cramer, had helpfully covered ground in advance. Benjamin Wright's caravan, would you believe it, had been open. 'No one's seen him for a couple of days,' he told Collier. 'But then, he often buggers off, so do they all.'

'And when he's here?'

'Like everyone else. Drinks. Gambles – one of these scrotes runs a card school. You won't bloody credit it – but one or two of them here play *bridge*. Straight up. Always thought that was for old ladies with money long past anything else. Mind you, any of this lot could come from anywhere, drop-outs from the highest and the lowest. Some of them talk dead posh.'

'Benjamin?'

'Yeah, by all accounts. Never came across him myself.'

'Did he have a car?'

'Seems not. But it's easy enough to get lifts from here, if you're not bothered where you're going. And what does it matter when you've bugger all else to do? He'd go to any of the towns anyone was going. Did the rounds of the boozers, the toms. Stocked up on pornographic magazines, videos . . .'

There were enough of those in the caravan, some unsavoury takeaways in the fridge but plenty of cans of beer, bottles of spirits. DC Walker said, 'When he's away doesn't anyone turn him over?'

'Regularly, I'd say. Par for the course. Who's he going to complain to? Won't call us in that's for sure.'

The shabby caravan showed signs of little care and a great deal of use, smelling of stale food and unwashed clothes. A painstaking search brought to light a false panel beneath the sink. There was a passport in the name of Benjamin Wright; the photograph showed a bespectacled man of indefinite age and such commonplace features he really would pass unnoticed in a crowd. There were also almost four hundred pounds in cash, and a creased, grubby piece of paper misspelling what passed for a letting agreement between himself and the manager of the site, who appeared in a dirty track suit, indignant.

'I never gave you lot no permission –'

'What can you tell us about Benjamin Wright?' Cramer asked.

'Nuthin'.'

'Thought not, piss off.' Cramer closed the door on him.

'If he'd stayed away much longer,' Collier said, bagging the find, 'this lot would have gone. It's hard to tell if anything else has, though.'

DS Walker said, 'If the door was open, anyone could have come in and we wouldn't know what –'

'Did I say open?' Cramer asked innocently. 'No, I was examining the lock and it must have been faulty, just sort of came undone –'

'All right,' Collier said. 'Do you think that manager really doesn't have anything to tell us about Benjamin?'

'He makes a point of never knowing anything, only way he can survive. I'll tell you what, if anyone had turned this place over, you'd know. It'd be in a bigger mess than it is now.'

That was true, what was amazing was that the typewriter had survived any previous break-ins, quite likely because no one knew what it was. An old manual, a Remington. How had Hunter known it would be here?

Cramer said, 'This guy – has he snuffed it?'

'Probably.'

Over five years ago.

*   *   *

After Collier had reported back, Hunter said to Annette, 'Right, let's put it all together before we see her again.'

They worked through the file. Annette, studying the pathologist's report, said, 'I don't know what Nella's QC reckons he's going to use for defence. Nothing in this, for sure.'

Hunter sounded a note of caution. 'I hope to God you're right, but we've got to keep on top of this to the bitter end; if Ms Lynchet can work it, she'll get some crafty brief to spring something when we're not looking. But, sure, that report just confirms what was already obvious. Benjamin was about to leave the garage, she came up behind him and hit him on the back of the head.'

'But she can't remember anything about the struggle, she's still too confused,' Annette quoted. 'That could be true, guv. It's common after a trauma. And the forensic evidence will prove what she did . . . but *why*? And what's the point in her insisting it was Benjamin when it can be proved it was Alfred? And everyone can testify she practically worshipped *him*.'

'Ms Lynchet remembers what she wants to remember, and believes what she wants to believe. God knows how long she can keep it up, though.' He paused, sat silent for a while, then said, 'Her brother did for over five years.'

Annette said, puzzled, 'What?'

'Being someone else.'

'He took Benjamin's name –'

'He did more than that. Look what Collier found. How he lived, a reversal of his entire life. No responsibilities, no social obligations, no need to earn his living, as much booze as he could drink and the kind of sex he could manage. He'd been hag-ridden by Grandmother since he was too young to defend himself. So he became someone else, like getting out of a straitjacket.'

'Until Jaynie tracked him down.'

'Didn't take much tracking. All she did was plunder Nella's papers when Nella had her accident.'

'Yes, but . . . why did she wait?'

'I don't think she could cope with more than one idea at a time, she wasn't very bright, poor woman.'

Annette said, 'All right, but she wasn't impetuous. Inez said she prepared unpleasant surprises and sprang them on people when she was ready. But, guv, if you remember, Nella was at great pains to point out that Jaynie couldn't have got Benjamin's address from her, she didn't have it, and we couldn't find it anywhere –'

'Except in Jaynie's research file. After a couple of years of sending him money every month Nella would have it engraved on her memory. I'm sure she kept a record of it, even so, just as I'm sure once Jaynie disappeared she destroyed it.'

'And, to make doubly sure, she pinched Jaynie's file.'

'And denied all knowledge of it. You remember how emphatic she was. *I have no idea what could be in the wretched thing.* That could be true. Because I don't think she looked. I think she needed to know for her own sake but she just couldn't bear to look – not now, not with everything that was going on. She could limit its damage as long as it was in her possession – I think she just shoved it in the back of a filing drawer and told herself it didn't exist.'

Annette said thoughtfully, 'Yes, I agree about that. But . . . is it the sort of thing she would do, off her own bat?'

'That's what I've been wondering. Did Alfred get in touch with her somehow while Jaynie was missing?'

They talked for a while, exploring possibilities, reaching tentative conclusions.

' . . . but no way did she know it was Alfred, because when he did turn up, he told her all sorts of things she didn't want to know.'

Hunter said, 'She'd become someone else, too. She had money, independence, status . . .'

'But only as long as he was dead.'

'And that's the "why?", isn't it? His life or hers.'

Annette thought of Nella: self-obsessed, arrogant, living at the dangerous interchange between reality and delusion. 'The trouble with the Lynchets, Inez told me, is that they've always believed themselves so superior no one has got the nous to question them. Just look what Grandmother got away with, for God's sake. Perjury, perverting the course of justice, aiding and abetting murder . . . No wonder with that role model Nella thinks we're going to accept this fantasy that she acted for the common good in ridding society of a murderer in the course of saving her own life.'

'That's why she has to keep insisting it was Benjamin – not her own brother – let loose, who's to say Alfred couldn't be found and charged with two murders. Then the name of Lynchet really would be in the mud.'

'Mmm. But none of that could be laid at Nella's door.'

'True. The fox and the hedgehog thing . . .'

'I don't think I'm even going to try and follow that.'

'No, don't. Just take it from me, what she had known for a long time she had to keep to herself, or her own world would come crashing down.'

Before they went to the interview room, Hunter received a message from the search team at Ferns. Concealed beneath generations of old documents at the bottom of a cupboard in the study they had found Jaynie's address book; the W section contained the name and address of Benjamin Wright.

'Nella's done it again,' Annette said. 'Over-confident. She just didn't look, any more than she looked in Jaynie's file.'

'She was following her instincts. If she kept herself in ignorance of what was in the file and the address book, we could ask till we were blue in the face. She could honestly say she didn't know.'

Chapter Twenty nine

Hunter said, 'I should like to talk to you about your brother's typewriter, Miss Lynchet.'

Beside the cowed and silent Mr Jelks, Nella, alert, immaculate, launched herself into what Hunter and Annette had come to recognise as one of her monologues: lengthy (if given the chance) and, in view of her circumstances, inappropriately self-satisfied.

'He was a meticulous craftsman. He always said the creative stage was not only cerebral, there was a tactile dimension – the energy from brain to pen. I often make a point of that in my talks on his technique. He never used the typewriter until everything was complete, ready to be –'

Annette said, 'I understand when Benjamin Wright first came to stay with you, your brother encouraged him to join in various local activities.'

'You must stop interrupting me, young woman. However, yes, Alfred was kindness itself. All wasted, Benjamin was just not – socially –'

Resolutely, Annette interrupted, 'Like the writers' group. Alfred encouraged him to write as a kind of therapy.'

Nella pursed her lips then, resigned, answered, 'Well, again he might just as well have saved his time. Benjamin never –'

'Exactly how did he encourage him? Did he read his work? Comment on it? Did they work together in the study?'

'Let me . . .' She put her hand to her brow. 'Let me try to remember, it was so long –'

Hunter said, 'Not so long ago, Miss Lynchet. You are an authority on your brother's working methods.'

'Indeed. I am widely known –'

'You told me it was eight years since Benjamin left. Why did you say that?'

She frowned, shook her head. 'I must have had my mind on something else.'

'It wasn't true, was it?'

'I can't be expected –'

'Your brother's typewriter – it was more or less a family heirloom – belonged to your parents.'

'Yes.'

'It isn't in the study now.' When she said nothing, he went on. 'How do you account for that?'

She would have worked something out since the last interview, but she made a show of pondering. 'I think . . . yes, I recall my grandmother saying . . . Alfred gave it to Benjamin when he went away. As a kind of keep-sake, an encouragement. A generous gesture typical of my brother.'

Having allowed her to complete a sentence, Annette said with interest, 'Really? But when Mr Hunter asked when Benjamin left, you got the time wrong. Because it was too long ago for you to remember accurately. Now you can remember, quite clearly, something that was told you at the time. Don't you think that's rather –'

'I will not be directed to think anything by you,' Nella said tartly.

'Benjamin never went anywhere, except to the crema-torium,' Hunter said. 'It was your brother who took the Remington away with him. To Brite Caravan Park, that's where we found it. In the caravan your brother has been living in, calling himself Benjamin Wright.'

'I know nothing of any caravan park.'

'Yes, you do. The address was in the address book you

removed from Mrs Turner's when you called there. Late. In the dark.'

'You can have no possible grounds for these accusations –'

'Her address book has been found in your study.'

'I don't care what that wretched woman has written where, nothing would ever induce me to read a word. If you have found – whatever – I can only assume it was because you put it where you could find it.'

'That's a serious accusation, Miss Lynchet. I would advise you to reconsider it. Meanwhile . . .' Hunter looked down at the papers on the table before him. Amongst them was DS Warren's report; no one except himself and Chief Superintendent Garrett had read it yet. 'Brite Caravan Park. You've been sending money there every month since your grandmother became too incapable to manage her affairs. Before that, she saw to the payments.'

Annette made the slightest movement which only Hunter could interpret as: *I knew you had something up your sleeve, you old hound.*

Nella was silent for a long moment before saying, 'You can prove nothing.'

No, they couldn't . . . Hunter studied the papers before him. DS Warren's first rapid assessment of some seemingly innocent figures had been confirmed by the Lynchets' bank. Shortly after Alfred's death, monthly withdrawals, in cash, from Mrs Lynchet's account, had increased by eight hundred pounds. Allowing for extras incurred by funeral and legal costs and suchlike, the pattern remained constant. Before Mrs Lynchet's death handling of all finances passed solely to Nella. Her change of lifestyle was evident in a leap in expenditure, a corresponding leap in income – but still the pattern continued.

You can prove nothing . . . Mr Jelks, having despairingly inclined towards Nella, recoiled from her glare. '. . . furthermore, I cannot believe that Mr Travis, who has been our bank manager for twenty years, would allow you examine –'

'He was obliged to, Miss Lynchet, once we obtained a warrant. I did wonder why you settled for paying Benjamin a generous amount of money, every month. After all, you didn't owe him anything.' He paused. 'Or did you?'

She turned from his gaze, stared at nothing.

'You believed, you had to believe, that as long as you went on paying him he would stay where he was. Very likely he would have done. Until Jaynie started making waves. Then you were both heading for exposure, weren't you? You, and your brother. Jaynie had written to him, he knew trouble was on the way. So he contacted you, didn't he?'

She sat as if she could not hear.

'He wouldn't phone, you'd recognise his voice, no matter how long it's been. So he wrote to you – "Benjamin" wrote to you. Told you to get rid of Benjamin's original manuscripts, plot summaries – anything. It must have given you quite a jolt when the letter arrived – recognising the lettering of the Remington – you know it so well.' Hunter put his pen down carefully, aligning it with the side of the paper nearest Annette.

Annette said, 'We have had a comparison made of the letters on the Remington – it's a distinctive old-fashioned type called pica – and your brother's manuscripts. The type matches, all the characteristics of wear and use match.'

In a contained, stubborn way, Nella said, 'I told you, Grandmother gave Alfred's typewriter to –'

'Of course,' Annette said, 'he would have phoned Jaynie – to arrange a meeting. She wasn't familiar with his voice, hadn't heard it for years. He wouldn't be so reckless as to put anything in writing to her.'

Hunter said thoughtfully, 'But in your study there was nothing in his handwriting. We have specimens for comparison – his signature on contracts, notes he made on letters to his agent. But the first drafts of manuscripts – no, there's nothing handwritten.'

She refused to look at him. 'Why should there be? His output was prodigious, he couldn't keep every scrap of paper.'

'Oh, I understood you to say he had. Your files contained – what was it? Plots, outlines, synopses? Which you said only a few moments ago he wrote by hand.' Consideringly, he picked up his pen, made a note.

Annette said, 'Benjamin was a withdrawn man, wasn't he, Miss Lynchet? After an initial attempt, he stopped mixing, avoided people altogether. He was content to be quiet at Ferns, gardening, reading, writing, listening to music, the radio – he disliked television, would never watch it, would he?' Primed by Hunter, she had not understood the significance of the question until now. Nella appeared not to have heard it.

Hunter said, 'So he didn't know anything about the Toddies, did he?' He placed no emphasis on the name but it was as if a whisper moved on the air, a despairing credulity that something so shoddy should generate violence, progress through fraud, murder and deception, to cause the death of a silly, innocent, meddling woman. 'He would have known, eventually, it was only a matter of time before he found out. That Alfred had stolen his creation, passed it off as his own, that your grandmother colluded in this. Benjamin became an embarrassment; he could pull the rug out from under the fantasy. Benjamin became expendable. Didn't he?' Hunter finished quietly.

Her voice subdued, Nella said, 'This is your fantasy, Mr Hunter –'

'No, it's yours now. Your grandmother told you about the plagiarism, you couldn't see you had any choice except to continue it. Now it's grown into your whole life.'

Increasingly shaken, Mr Jelks intervened. 'I really must have a word in private with my client.'

Hunter said, 'Miss Lynchet. Do you wish me to suspend the interview?'

She sat like a rock. But he knew her by now, knew by a darting in the eyes that would not meet his that her brain was busy.

She began to speak, still subdued, but matter-of-fact. 'I have admitted from the outset that I was forced to kill Benjamin Wright, a double murderer, in defence of my own life and for the good of society. I shall pay the penalty the law requires – Mr Jelks has assured me it will not be too harsh, in view of the circumstances. But I am familiar with the insatiable interest of the public; when I am at liberty Ferns will be besieged, I shall be – doorstepped, I believe is the expression. I shrink from publicity. It will be necessary for you to provide some protection . . .'

Annette sat briefly dazed until her mind nudged into a mental replay of her arrival at Ferns with the murder team. A beautifully turned-out, dignified, if shocked Nella waited . . . It hadn't registered then, in the urgency of the moment: Nella had given herself time to destroy papers, lock others away, but she had done more than was necessary to protect herself, she had *set the scene*, even dressed for it. Waited . . . to give an audience.

Later, outside in the corridor, Annette was vehement. 'Can I *believe* what I heard? Does she expect *us* to believe all that – that play-acting – that –'

'Calm down, girl,' Hunter said gently.

'Guv, how can you be so – This is how she's going to try and get off. That business – how dare she – about us planting Jaynie's address book on her.'

'You've got her measure, she's going to accuse us of just about everything except sexual harassment – hang about, probably that. She knows just what to admit to, what to deny.'

'Yes, and think what a clever brief can do with it –

she's admitted to murder and – and – turned herself into a heroine.'

'No, she's claimed self-defence and turned herself into a heroine. There's a hell of a difference between that and admitting Alfred faced a criminal charge for strangling a prostitute because he was impotent, ran down a friend and stole his identity, lived off the proceeds of his efforts and then murdered a harmless woman who had no idea what she was doing.'

'Look, she tried to rig the evidence before we got to Ferns – she didn't even do that properly –'

'Of course she didn't, she was too shocked. She had been betrayed for years by Alfred, her whole existence was in jeopardy. She did a damage limitation – not enough; she thought she was being clever, but she wasn't clever enough. She's desperate and pathetic and close to the edge. I pity her, but I'm not going to let her get away with anything. Come on, Annette, we've got a job to do.'

Chapter Thirty

Inez had a phone call from Mrs Hanks' sister. 'Her cold's that much worse, she's taken a really bad turn. It's her breathing.'

'Oh, I am sorry, I'm afraid I've been rather –'

'They've got her in St Luke's. So I told her I'd ask you –'

'Of course, I'll –'

'She worries about that dog. She said you'd not mind. Having him. Only it's my husband, never been able to abide dogs . . .'

He's not the only one. Inez's mind went into hold while she received instructions, eventually managing to send her best wishes and promise to visit Mrs Hanks. Then she got out her car and drove up to Regatta Terrace. The kitchen door was unlocked; the armadillo rushed out into the back garden; he'd been shut in for some time. When he came back and was greeting her in a quiet, fretful way, she collected his bed, his box of toys, his bag of doggy food and his brush. 'Come on, old chap, everything'll be all right, you'll see. You're going to be my lodger for a while.'

Back at her cottage, she settled him in. The phone began to ring. She ignored it, she was fed up with the phone ringing. News of the sensational events at Ferns had reached Joe's relatives – mercifully quiescent of late – who were cramming her answering machine with demands to know *everything* and should several dozen of them pop along to keep her company? As the only possible response to that was *I'd rather kill myself* she just kept deleting the messages. Clerehaven was reverberating with wild stories that were not, Inez reflected ruefully, anywhere near as wild as the truth – whatever that was, she was no longer sure herself. She had to keep making the effort to adjust her mind to the grotesque image of old Mrs Lynchet, with her eagle-beaked face and black clothes, upright as a monument, looking at Benjamin's dead face and declaring him to be her own son. If only Hunter had not told her, but she understood why he had; with that knowledge she had no choice but to agree to identify Alfred.

One welcome call was from Dora, still at the Wirral. Inez hadn't phoned, not wanting to bother her, and she was still obviously very upset about her lost grandchild. They talked for a while, sadly. When everything necessary had been said, Inez asked, 'About Nella – do you want chapter and verse, Door?'

'No, you can tell me all about it when I get back. I just rang to make sure you're all right, Index. It must be awful for you.'

'No, honestly. I'm OK.'

'Sure? I'm not there to regulate you, but you've got Sam.'

'Yes.' Due back from his course today. If she could work out what today was.

'And Evelina.'

'Absolutely.' Evelina's large house was bursting with relatives staying for some anniversary. 'Don't bother about me, Door, I'm fine.'

She had a cup of tea, and the armadillo a saucer of milk with a colouring of tea and a chocolate biscuit as a treat. He ignored it. 'Listen, you're something of a hero. You made a citizen's arrest or something. Well, nearly. You *might* get a medal. How about that? Oh, all right . . . Well, I can tell you, I'm not having much of a time myself. What about we go and see if Sam's home?'

When they turned into the street of neat Victorian

houses where Sam lived, the armadillo's head went up and his tail gave something like a wag; but Inez could see a car had approached from the other direction and pulled up outside Sam's house. She paused and stood in the shelter of a large holly, unseen. James Collier got out of the car and Sam's door opened; from the look on his face he wouldn't have seen her if she'd been doing handstands in the middle of the road. 'Oh, well, we'll make ourselves scarce for the present, maybe phone later . . .' she said to the armadillo.

They went for a walk, turning for home as the short day drew to a close and Clerehaven settled to a winter evening of lamplight and firelight, sherry and supper and television. The telephone rang as Inez took off her coat. She had no intention of playing back her messages but just to settle her conscience and in case it was something important, she picked up the phone.

'Hallo, Inez,' Hunter said.